CHANGED FATE

A LOVE STORY ACROSS TIME

LANCE STOUFFER

HEATHROW PUBLISHING

Changed Fate

A Love Story Across Time

By

Lance Stouffer

John,
Keep Dreaming!
Lance
Oct. 2012

This book is a work of fiction. Names, characters, places and incidents are products of the author's imagination or are used fictitiously. Any resemblance to actual events or locales or persons, living or dead is entirely coincidental.

A Heathrow Publishing book, Heathrow, Florida

heathrowpublishing@cfl.rr.com

Second publishing May 2012, with bonus materials.

DC-3 drawing courtesy of A. Whitlock

Cover designed by Brian E. Bourke

ISBN-13: 978-0-578-01341-1

To all you lovers and dreamers out there.

You know who you are!

Love is a funny, powerful and complex emotion; it knows no constraints or bounds including time. When the spirits of two are united in love across time there is still little that can get in the way. Even fate knows when to step aside ….

Author

PART ONE

Chapter 1 – Chicago, Illinois, Friday, May 23, 1952, 10 am

"Taxi please, Sam," Nan told the doorman of the Palmer House where she had been staying.

"Where to Miss?" he asked.

"Midway Airport," she replied.

The doorman, dressed in a dark green uniform, blew his whistle and started hailing a cab. Looking up, she heard the sound of an elevated train rumbling into the Adams Street station. She heard the squeal of brakes as the train stopped. Soon people from the train started to descend the stairs next to the hotel. Nan's eyes followed a young woman, about her age, heading her way and wondered from appearances what her city life was like. As the woman approached, Nan glanced at her left hand to see if a ring was present. No ring. She was attractive and Nan wondered why, in the big city of Chicago, she appeared to be alone. Finally, a Checker cab appeared at the curb. Nan's bags were loaded into the trunk and she slipped a tip into Sam's hand.

"See you again Sam, and thanks," Nan said as she climbed into the rear seat.

The door closed and the journey to Chicago's Midway Airport began. Nan smiled; it had been a wonderful week in Chicago with her father, Paul Orland, owner of Denver-based Orland Cattle Company, which was the largest cattle company in Colorado. Working with her father as business manager was a natural thing for her. She had been raised on the family's cattle ranch just outside of Denver and loved the outdoor life, including the beautiful mountain views and sunny days, especially at this time of year. Horseback riding and cattle ranching were a part of her very soul. She opened her handbag to get a cigarette and pulled out a Kool menthol, lit up and eyed the large blue ribbon inside her purse that said Best of Show, 1952 Chicago International Stockman's Exposition. This made her very proud and a smile formed on her face. The award confirmed that Orland beef was of the finest quality. More business would surely follow and this reminded her that the new Swift contract needed reading on the plane. Topper, the winning bull, had been raised especially for the show under Nan's supervision.

"Miss," the cab driver said, "we'll go down the South Shore Drive and cut over at 55th Street to save time."

Nan knew a little about Chicago, but mostly by accompanying her father on the train from Denver, his preferred mode of transport.

"Fine" she replied, not really knowing if this was the best route.

Her father was staying the weekend as guest of Johnny Miller, owner of Miller's Steakhouse on Rush Street. Miller was the highest bidder on their prize bull at the charity auction dinner Wednesday night and Topper was now proudly on display in front of his restaurant. Chicago tradition always had the winning bull auctioned off to a restaurant or hotel in Chicago and the bidding was very competitive, yet fun at the same time. Topper would not turn into a steak, not just yet, as he was just on loan to the winning restaurant to promote their steak house; he would eventually come home to Denver.

Nan and her father had dined at Miller's Steakhouse last night and Nan said goodbye to Topper. She thought it curiously funny to have the bull penned in front of the steakhouse, with searchlights going round and round, but this was Chicago in 1952. Mayor Kennelly also attended the celebration dinner and the press took tons of publicity photos outside with everyone standing near the pen. What fun!

"Did you have a good stay in Chicago?" the cabby asked.

"Indeed, it's been lively fun all week," Nan replied.

The cab continued to roll down South Shore Drive, and she could hardly believe the past five exciting days in Chicago: attending the Exposition, winning best of show, seeing business friends, all the publicity and still having time for shopping on State Street. She loved to visit Chicago, an all-beef town!

This was her first airplane trip and some apprehension existed in her mind. She enjoyed train travel, and had it not been for an early morning event in Denver she had to attend, she would have taken the train home. However, the plane trip was a new adventure, would save her lots of time and maybe she would like it after all.

Nan looked at her left hand and brushed her right hand fingers over where a wedding ring should be. She tried to stop thinking about this, to always change the subject in her mind, but her gaze out the window at the blue water of Lake Michigan somehow made her run through this mental exercise again. At 26, Nan had dated quite a few men, but nothing had lead to anything serious. College was fun, she remembered with another smile, all the dances, parties, and football games. Maybe if she hadn't been chairman of so many of those events, she would have had time to really enjoy them and meet Mr. Right. True love had eluded her then, and continued to do so now. Why is it so complicated, she lamented to herself.

Nan's personality sparkled and those that were close to her knew her as bubbly and joyful. Her giggly laugh was infectious and everyone who met her instantly took a liking to her. The paragraph under her cameo picture in the 1947 University of Denver yearbook described her as tall, smart, focused, perky and fun to be with. Her friend Edwin, who was on the yearbook staff, had written that description and it fit, or so she thought. Most of it, anyway, but was it still true today, she wondered?

At five foot ten, Nan was tall, well proportioned and fit. Her brown hair was styled in a trendy under-tuck curl. Maybe her size intimidated men, she thought. Also, a smart, college-educated businesswoman in 1952 was a rarity. Her gift at truly understanding business affairs and her organizational skills made her a natural to help her father in the cattle company offices. Combining her loves of the outdoors and ranching with her astute business sense, assisting with running the back office of the cattle business made sense to her. Somehow finance and accounting came easy to her, and her father couldn't be more pleased to have her working in the business.

She enjoyed meeting people and had the gift of putting them immediately at ease. She knew that her height gave her great immediate presence, her looks captured attention and then she followed up with her wry intellect. She was a quipster, like her father, and her one-liners always got a smile from someone. She remembered somewhere reading about brains and beauty. She had the brains part, she knew, but the beauty part, well, she never really knew how it was measured. Eventually, her logic always concluded that if she had so much going for her, why couldn't she find Mr. Right?

"We're about 15 minutes away from Midway," the cabby barked, as they were now headed west on 55th street.

"Thanks, and United Airlines, please," Nan replied.

Soon the Checker cab glided to the curb in front of the terminal building. A porter opened the cab door for Nan and the cabbie headed back to the trunk. She handed the cabbie four dollars as the porter took her bags from the trunk and placed them on his cart.

"United 77 to Denver," she said to the porter and then headed into the airport lobby.

Chapter 2

Walking up to the United Airlines counter, she handed her ticket to the agent. Behind him the sign read United 77 Chicago to Denver leaving at 1:00 pm, Gate A. The porter placed her bags on the scales. New clothes from Marshall Field's were stuffed inside that she couldn't wait to wear.

"You're overweight! That's fifteen dollars extra, miss," the agent said.

Nan had never heard anyone say that to her before and she stared back at him, not knowing what to say. The agent repeated himself, this time clarifying his statement.

"Your bags are over the weight limit," he said. "We charge one dollar a pound over forty pounds."

"Oh, of course," she replied with an embarrassed smile and then reached into her handbag for her new ATC air travel card, knowing that the airline would send the overweight bill to the company in Denver. Wouldn't it be great to have one small card like this for everything you buy, she thought.

"Here's your boarding card, miss," the agent said, handing her card and ticket folder back. "We're forty five minutes to boarding at Gate A."

Nan placed the ticket and ATC card back in her handbag and smiled again at the agent. She turned and had begun to walk away when the porter tapped her on the shoulder.

"Miss, oh miss," he said.

She instantly remembered she hadn't tipped him. She stopped and reached into her handbag for her purse, snapped it open and grabbed all the change she had, four quarters, and gave it to him.

"Sorry," she said.

"Thank you very much, miss," he replied, as he touched his hat in a salute and walked away.

"Girl," she said in a soft voice, "I think a martini would taste good now, but a cup of coffee will do just fine."

Spotting the coffee shop sign, she walked up the stairs to the Cloud Room and sat next to the window overlooking the field. She ordered a cup of coffee. On the table was a copy of the *Chicago Tribune* that bore the headline 'Korean War Enters Second Year.' She remembered how she felt when the telegram had been delivered announcing that her older brother Ken had been killed in France on June 14, 1944, following the D-Day invasion. This broke the family's heart and never did she or her mother cry more tears than on that day. She remembers her father, about to cry, but he stiffened up, went outside, lit up a long Cuban cigar he had been saving and began walking around the ranch. All the plans they had for Ken after the war were gone in an instant. Nan loved her big brother, who enjoyed tickling her until she cried laughing tears. They slowly came back to normal family life, but she remembered that his room was left untouched for over a year with the door closed. She guessed this gave some solace to mom and dad, in case it was all a mistake and Ken was in there studying or reading or listening to music or something; that if they just opened the door he would be there. But when the door was opened it was always the same. Ken was not there. She remembered coming home from college for a weekend visit; the room was vacant with painters working on it. "Our new guest room," her mother said to her at the time. Life moves on, even in the Orland family, but his death was something they never quite forgot or really got over.

"United Flight 77 departing for Omaha and Denver now boarding at Gate A," blared from the PA speaker. It continued to announce, "All ticketed passengers should proceed to Gate A."

Nan paid for her coffee, got up and went to the lobby and towards Gate A. She handed her ticket to the gate agent and walked out the door and across the tarmac to the waiting plane.

"So this is the new Super DC-3 dad said I would be flying on," she said, softly approaching the plane.

She remembered him telling her it was an upgraded, newer version of the pre-war plane, but faster and more luxurious. She liked all those words, especially new and fast.

Chapter 3

The sun was bright and it reflected off the bare, polished aluminum of the new Super DC-3 making the fuselage almost glow. Nan climbed the steps and was greeted by the planes stewardess in her neat blue suit and cap. She noticed the gold wings on her coat with the words United Airlines in the center. Underneath was a name tag that read Kimm.

"Miss Orland?" the stewardess asked.

"Yes, I am," she answered. They both smiled at each other.

"Welcome aboard. Seat 5A on your left, please."

Nan walked up the inclined aisle to her seat, remembering her father affectionately calling these planes tail draggers, as the only time everything was level was in flight. She placed her handbag and valise on the aisle seat and slid into 5A, the window seat. The other passengers boarding along with her took their seats and eventually the exit door closed. A speaker near the front of the cabin came to life.

"Ladies and gentlemen, welcome aboard United Flight 77, all first class Super DC-3 service to Omaha and Denver. I am Captain Eric Jamison with first officer Mark Palmer in the right seat. Miss Laura Kimm is your stewardess today. Please fasten your seatbelts and extinguish any cigarettes as we'll be departing momentarily. Flight control says we have clear skies all the way to Omaha."

Looking out the window, Nan saw the left engine propeller starting to turn. Soon, the engine coughed to life, with smoke appearing under the wing. Nan felt the engine vibration through the floor and seat and it doubled as the right engine started. The cabin was a little noisy with the engines running. A ground crewman looking at the pilot pointed out to the runway and the plane began to move. The powerful engines of the Super DC-3 went faster, then slowed. In a few minutes the plane sat at the end of the runway. The stewardess walked up the aisle looking at everyone's seatbelts to be sure they were fastened. She then retreated to her jump seat in the rear of the aircraft. Captain Jamison stood on the brakes at the end of runway 22 and brought the engines up to take-off power. Taking his foot off the brakes the Super DC-3 launched down the runway, lifting effortlessly into the sky. Nan said goodbye to Chicago through the window as the plane climbed into the bright afternoon sky and headed west.

In the cockpit, Captain Jamison ordered the landing gear up, which co-pilot Palmer immediately did. Cruising speed for the flight was 220 knots.

"We'll make Omaha by three-thirty," Jamison said to Palmer.

Nan noticed that the cabin had leveled off and the other passengers were going about their business, looking out the windows, reading or talking. She looked out her window at the green checkerboard farm fields below and marveled how far she could see of the flat Illinois landscape. It was a beautiful day and she now knew flying was a wonderful way to travel. She thought the engine vibration and engine droning sounds were kind-of soothing and relaxing. Soon Stewardess Laura Kimm came up the aisle handing out newspapers, magazines and beverages. Nan asked for a copy of *Life* magazine and placed it on the seat next to her to read later; first, she wanted to work on the contract. She opened her valise, pulled out the Swift contract and started to read. This was a big deal that would put their company on the map. She read the words over and over that called for a two-year agreement totaling four million pounds of beef per year. A tall order, but they could do it. We'll have to expand our ranching operation and perhaps buyout some of our competitors, Nan thought to herself.

An hour into the flight, Captain Jamison appeared at the front of the cabin and began to nod and smile to each passenger. When he reached Nan, he looked at her and said hello, and touched the tip of his hat. She smiled and nodded hello right back. Nan thought he looked great in his blue uniform, with gold wings on his breast pocket and gold hash marks on his sleeves. Jamison was forty-five years old and an eighteen-year veteran with United Airlines. As Captain Jamison turned to greet the women across the aisle, Nan noticed that she remained expressionless, barely making eye contact with him. Nan continued to look at the woman as Jamison walked past. What a somber, almost sullen face, Nan thought. Then, the woman turned toward the window and stared out. Not too friendly, Nan thought, but each to his own. Stewardess Kim walked by and noticed Nan staring at the woman across the aisle. She stopped and leaned over to Nan and whispered that she had just lost her husband in Korea. Now it made more sense. Nan remembered for the second time today her frame of mind when the news of her brother's death reached her. However, she knew this situation was quite different.

"Oh, how sad," Nan said to the stewardess before she continued up the aisle.

For unknown reasons, she immediately put down the Swift contract, slid over into the seat next to her and tapped the woman in seat 5C. She introduced herself.

"I am Nan Orland and am very sorry for your loss. I lost my brother during the last war," she said. "If you want to talk, I'm happy to listen."

The woman looked at Nan and nodded.

"Let me come over next to you," the woman replied.

Nan returned to her seat and the woman sat down next to Nan.

"My name is Joan Lorry. My husband John was killed in Korea last week and I don't know what to do. I loved him so much. We were married less than a year ago and were going to start a family when he returned from Korea."

She continued to tell Nan they knew they were meant for each other from the first time they met and that they had lived their love for each other every day.

"Now I don't see a future," Joan said.

Nan turned towards her and said in a comforting way that everything would be fine, that better times in her life were just ahead! She knew her words sounded hollow and could not fill the current void in Joan's life, but she knew what a grieving person wanted to hear. Joan's red, teary eyes would not change from anything that Nan said. It's as if they would be that way forever. Losing a spouse is so much different than a brother, Nan concluded. She could see in Joan's empty eyes her lost dreams and dashed possibilities. Joan thanked Nan for caring and listening to her. Nan had a thousand questions to ask, but the words would not come out.

"Everything will be alright," she told Joan. "You'll see."

Joan then got up and returned to her seat across the aisle and continued to gaze out the window at the blue sky with a blank, thousand mile stare so familiar to combat veterans; she saw nothing but her own despair in the bright sunlight.

Nan picked up the Swift contract again and continued to read it, but her concentration was gone for now. She could not get Joan's emotions out of her mind that quickly. A final jotted note in the contract margin and she placed it back into her valise. Picking up the *Life* magazine did not clear her mind either. She knew that Joan had found her true love, and had been living her love, but now their future dreams were gone. Nan knew the personal questions she wanted to ask were inappropriate. In her mind was the question of how Joan knew her husband was the one, the elusive 'thing' that brings a relationship together. Could Joan reveal to her what it was? Nan had never felt the true love that Joan had. Both women had emptiness in their lives because of love, but Joan's current emptiness was closer to Grand Canyon size.

Captain Jamison's voice came over the speaker, announcing their approach to Omaha; they would be on the ground in about one hour. He then mentioned that the airport coffee shop served the best coffee and it was complimentary to all United Airlines passengers.

The plane slowly descended during its approach to Omaha. Nan watched out the window as the ground grew closer and closer. Soon the announcement was made to fasten seatbelts for landing; Nan fastened her belt. She could feel the landing gear shifting to its down and locked position with a bump. The

Super DC-3 descended and made a perfect landing at the Omaha Municipal Airport. Captain Jamison taxied the plane to the front of the terminal building and shut down the engines. Nan waited in her seat until all the other passengers had de-planed. Walking down the aisle to the exit door, she was greeted by Stewardess Kimm telling her to watch her head and step. Nan exited the DC-3 and walked across the tarmac toward the terminal.

Chapter 4

The Omaha terminal building was small compared to Chicago's Midway Airport, and had none of the hustle and bustle. Nan walked slowly through the lobby and into the coffee shop. Looking around, there was only one vacant seat at the counter. She noticed Joan sitting on the next stool. Nan sat down and said hello. Joan appeared more composed than she had on the plane and even found a brief smile as she said the pie she was nibbling on was very good. Invariably, Joan again started talking to Nan about her husband and all the plans they had when he got out of the Army. They were going to buy a house, raise kids and grow old together.

"If he hadn't been recalled to duty for two years, he would be alive today," Joan said. "He was a radar repairman during World War II and the Army desperately needed him back. We met a year ago while he was home on leave from his training station in Ft. Monmouth, New Jersey."

"How did you meet? Nan asked.

"Oh, that was so much fun. It was at a dance at the Plantation Dinner Club in downtown Denver."

"Yes, I know the place," Nan replied.

"He asked me to dance and that was it. One look into his eyes and I knew he was for me. We got married right away and then he had to leave for Korea. We've been writing to each other every day and making plans for the day he would come home and our lives together would begin. Damn the Army. Damn the war. What do I have to live for now?" she exclaimed.

At that point, Joan began to tear up and her voice cracked; her somber and sullen appearance returned. Then, the loudspeaker announced that the flight to Denver was now boarding. Nan took another sip of coffee as Joan quietly got up and left the coffee shop without saying another word. She held her handkerchief up to her eyes to absorb the tears. Nan finished her coffee, got up and hurried out of the coffee shop to the gate.

Nan figured that Joan needed a timeout from her emotions, and their brief encounter in the coffee shop was that time. Nan sensed correctly that Joan had found Mr. Right and that an invisible, invincible bond had been permanently created between them. Her new husband's tragic war death left Joan cut open and unfulfilled. Nan tried to understand what was going on and thought rationally that Joan would finally say to herself, oh well, he's dead, let's move on to the next chapter in my life. Somehow, Nan knew it was probably not that easy to rationalize. This was a devastating personal loss for Joan and that for whatever reason she could not cope or deal with in a normal way. Grief is a very strong emotion that can consume your very being if left inside. It must come out, which is normal and then time can heal the wounded soul.

As Nan approached the plane she could see Joan boarding up ahead and Stewardess Kimm standing by the boarding stairs.

"Welcome back, Miss Orland," she greeted Nan with a pleasant smile. "Did you enjoy your brief stay in Omaha?"

"Why of course," she replied.

"Then this way to Denver," she said pointing to the door. "Watch you step, please."

Nan re-took her seat and glanced over to Joan, who was staring out the window again. Leave her alone, Nan thought to herself. She reached down and inserted the seatbelt latch into the buckle assembly and heard the 'click' that it was fastened. She felt secure in her seat.

"This is your captain speaking." Jamison's voice crackled from the speaker. "We'll be off on our final leg to Denver's Stapleton Airfield momentarily. Please be sure your seatbelts are securely fastened. We're expecting clear skies and normal headwinds all the way to Denver. The weather boys say that thunderstorms are predicted later in the evening, but we'll be on the ground long before then. First Officer Palmer and I again thank you for flying United Airlines. Enjoy your flight!"

Soon the engines started and Nan watched the ramp choreography again, with the ground crewman waving the plane out to the runway. Stewardess Kimm made her rounds to ensure each passenger was buckled in. In another few minutes the plane was sitting at the end of the runway. Then the engines went to full speed and United 77 was in the air again, headed west toward Denver.

Chapter 5

Nan pulled the Swift contract out of her valise again and picked up where she'd left off before. After half an hour, her eyes drifted from the page and she put the contract down on her lap. The plane's vibration and the droning sound of the engines made her want to doze off; fatigue from the hectic week was catching up with her. Even coffee could not keep her awake. She closed her eyes. Her mind slowly began to think about Joan and then it focused on the certain void in her own life, however, she was too tired to think about all of it further and in the next instant she dozed off.

Nan woke to Stewardess Kimm tapping her on the shoulder. She turned to see the stewardess sitting next to her, holding a glass of water.

"I hope you had a nice nap, Miss Orland? We'll be landing soon and I thought you might like a glass of water," she said.

Nan took the glass and sipped the water.

"Oh, thanks so much," Nan said. "It seems my week in Chicago really caught up with me."

Nan took another sip and handed the glass back to the stewardess, who then moved up the aisle. Nan placed the Swift contract back into her valise and looked out the window at the fluffy white clouds floating in the blue sky.

"Hello from the flight deck," the speaker blared. "I have been notified by Denver control that the thunderstorms we were expecting later in the evening are moving faster into Denver than originally anticipated. I expect some bumpy air ahead of the storm, but we'll be safely on the ground before it reaches Stapleton Airfield. Please return to your seats and fasten your seatbelts in preparation for landing. We'll be on the ground in approximately thirty minutes," Captain Jamison finished saying.

Nan then felt the plane shake softly as it headed into the outer headwinds of the storm. Soon the soft rolling was interspaced with stronger ups and downs of the roller coaster variety, but all seemed normal. She appreciated what Captain Jamison was doing to steady the plane and get them on the ground safe and sound. She looked out the window and saw grayer skies ahead of the plane. Looking around the cabin, all the passengers seemed to be going about their business as usual. Stewardess Kimm moved up and down the aisle, gathering cups and glasses; she appeared to be a pro at balancing herself and smiling at the same time. All was normal, or so Nan thought.

Chapter 6

Captain Eric Jamison made his approach to Denver's Stapleton Airfield as he had done many times before, landing north to south on runway one eight. This would be another routine landing added to his eighteen years of flying experience with United Airlines, except for the war years, where he flew B-17s over Germany. He was looking forward to a nice steak dinner with his crew once they were on the ground. In the morning he would fly the new Super DC-3 back to Chicago with a full passenger load.

The black clouds ahead gave him some concern that they were cutting it close before the storm hit the field, but it was nothing to really worry about. He was sure that they would be on the ground parked in front of the terminal before the rain started. He and Palmer finished going through the landing checklist; the plane was ready.

At five-fifty pm and ten minutes to touchdown he radioed the tower.

"Denver tower," he said into the microphone, "this is United 77 descending for final on one eight."

"Roger United 77," the tower controller responded. "We see you and you are clear on one eight. Be advised you are just ahead of a thunderstorm with winds gusting 20 to 30 knots from the south. We've got some rain drops starting here."

"Roger that," Captain Jamison replied as he un-keyed the microphone and looked over at Palmer.

"Damn, we're not going to beat this storm by much," he said.

Palmer looked over and replied "Cutting it close is our specialty, Cap."

Six miles to touchdown and at 1600 feet, the plane continued to descend and began to roll gently in the gusty headwinds. The first drop of rain hit the windshield in front of Jamison, and then another and another. He switched on the electric wipers that swept across both windshields.

"Remember those vacuum-actuated wipers in the old model DC-3?" he asked, looking over at Mark, who nodded. "They never worked when you needed them."

It was pitch black in front of the plane, but still daylight to the right and left. The Super DC-3 continued its descent.

"Can you see anything down there?" Jamison said.

"Nothing yet," replied Palmer.

Checking the directional finder and radar, Palmer confirmed to Jamison they were on the glide path five by five.

"Flaps 20 and gear down," Jamison commanded.

Palmer moved the flap lever to the second notch and hit both gear down levers. The hydraulic booster pump behind his seat kicked in with its usual high-pitched whine as the gear locked into place. Airspeed was 105 mph with the plane descending through 1300 feet. The drag of the flaps and lowered landing gear slowed the Super DC-3 too much and Captain Jamison pushed the throttles forward a bit. The twin Wright radial engines responded immediately, restoring the proper landing speed.

"There's the outer marker beacon, four miles to touchdown!" exclaimed Palmer.

Ground lights began to appear. The Stapleton Airfield tower's rotating beacon could now be seen in the distance. Jamison had beaten many a storm to the ground over the years and this would be just another. Three miles to touchdown and descending through 1000 feet, the runway lights also came into view. At one mile to touchdown the plane continued to pitch and roll in the wind, with Jamison and Palmer both now fighting the steering yoke and pedals to keep the plane in trim and on its decent. Jamison pulled back on the throttles and adjusted the propeller pitch controls. They were 300 feet above the ground moving through 100 mph when Jamison ordered Palmer to apply full flaps.

The Super DC-3 entered the front of the storm, a quarter-mile shy of the runway. Jamison felt the plane's descent stopping and a glance at the altimeter confirmed the plane was somehow gaining altitude. Then it began a sharp rise.

"Hey, what's going on?" he shouted to Palmer. "Our airspeed is dropping, but we're going up."

His eighteen years of flying experience came immediately into play. Instinctively, Captain Jamison rammed the throttles full forward to the emergency position.

"Full rich," he shouted as Palmer pushed the carburetor mixture control levers forward, bringing the engines to full emergency power.

"We'll climb out and bring her around for another go," Jamison shouted as he pulled the yoke back, but that was not to be.

At exactly six pm United 77 was over the end of the runway at 70 mph when the wind shear downdraft effect pushed the plane down. The engines straining at full power could do nothing against the overwhelming force of the downdraft. In seconds the plane's belly smacked down hard on the runway after falling over 100 feet. The plane made a short bounce back into the air then landed for good. The superior construction of the Super DC-3 kept it all together during the actual crash, but it now skidded straight down the runway. The initial impact burst both tires and pushed the landing gear struts through the top of the wings, rupturing the engine control cables, electrical, hydraulic and fuel lines. Both propellers began to saw into the concrete, curling, and one of the right propeller blades shattered, sending a two foot piece of metal through the aluminum fuselage into the cockpit, hitting and instantly killing first officer Palmer. The plane skidded down the runway, leaving a trail of sparks even in the rain. Slowly, the plane began to spin ever so slightly to the left until the right wing was pointing down the runway like a spear. After they had passed the Stapleton Airfield control tower, the plane began to drift to the right side of the runway and then it veered right onto the tarmac. The cockpit alarm buzzers were sounding and the instrument panel lights were flashing on battery power. Captain Jamison, shaken but unscathed from the crash, could do nothing but clutch the steering yoke and wait for the ride to be over. Looking out the right window he saw a truck in the distance rapidly approaching. The words TEXACO printed on the side of the truck came into view.

"Oh shit," Jamison uttered as the right wing sliced through the aviation gas tanker. He could feel the fuel truck slide up the wing and now both the plane and truck were intertwined in a dance of death. Gas washed over the wing and the right nose area of the fuselage and began to leave a trail behind the plane.

"This is not good," Jamison muttered.

The sparks from the plane's skid and the spilled aviation gas now met and lit up the tarmac area as the plane and fuel truck continued their death slide.

What seemed like an eternity to Jamison was in reality only seconds; the Super DC-3 finally came to rest. It was now raining hard, but that didn't make a difference to the trail of flames that soon caught up with the stopped plane. Captain Jamison unbuckled his three-point safety harness, got up and reached over to check his co-pilot, but Mark Palmer was clearly dead, the propeller shard imbedded in his right side. The aviation gas on the right wing and plane's front was now ablaze. Inside the cockpit it was like daylight from the orange flame of the gas fire. Jamison touched Palmer's shoulder gently, saying goodbye to his old friend, and moved back to the cabin through the cockpit door. There was no time for remorse.

Entering the cabin, Jamison quickly established that his passengers had not all faired well in the crash. Many appeared unconscious and the screams and cries for help from the conscious passengers were immediate and puzzling; those able to escape should be heading for the exit door, he thought. His training told him there was plenty of time to escape safely and he at first believed all could be rescued.

Twenty year-old Stewardess Kimm made it through the crash shaken but unharmed and was performing her first plane evacuation drill for real. She had the passenger door open by the time Jamison reached the passenger cabin and she could see the green grass just two feet below in the light of the brightly flickering flames. She pulled the woman from seat 7C first, escorted her to the door and told her to jump and run. As calmly as possible she did the same for the passengers in seats 7A and 7B, in the row just in front of the exit door. The two passengers in the next row up the aisle had freed themselves from their seatbelts and stumbled to the rear door, and with Laura's help exited the plane.

"Jump and run," she told them. "Jump and run."

At the same time, Captain Jamison tried to unbuckle the unconscious passenger in the first row, seat 1C, but the buckle would not release no matter how hard he tried to push the button and pull on the lap belts. Many of the conscious passengers had the same experience. They could not get the buckles to release and were shouting for help. Jamison realized this was trouble, as everyone could be evacuated quickly if they weren't trapped in their seats by their seatbelts.

Smoke was now beginning to fill the cabin, which was illuminated only by the fire outside. The faces of the passengers locked into their seats showed panic and the cries for help became more intense. "Free me, free me, help me!" exclaimed the passenger in seat 4A. "I can't get this damn buckle open!"

"Don't worry," Captain Jamison shouted from the cabin front. "Help is on the way. Please stay calm."

The words rolled instinctively from his mouth from all his training, but he knew help wouldn't be arriving anytime soon.

Nan Orland, in seat 5A, made it through the crash only shaken. She remained conscious for the entire traumatic ordeal. The thrashing around in her seat seemed to her no worse than being thrown from her horse, which had occurred many times growing up, though she thought the strong seatbelts and thick seat cushions also had something to do with her good fortune of not being injured. Now she was struggling with the buckle release button on her seatbelt. It would not release and she began begging for help along with everyone else. She continued to push the release button on the belt buckle but nothing happened. She looked up and saw Captain Jamison walk past carrying an unconscious man.

"Help me," she pleaded.

"Right back," he responded and continued down the aisle and out of the plane, placing the unconscious passenger from seat 3B on the grass. Why his seatbelt unbuckled normally when others wouldn't was a mystery. He then turned around and went back into the burning plane.

Racing back up the aisle he could see Stewardess Kimm at the front of the cabin trying to get the remaining passengers unbuckled, but to no avail. She glanced at him and shook her head. In the background he could finally hear fire truck sirens.

"Hang on everyone, help is almost here!" he shouted.

The cabin smoke was now making it hard to breathe; it burned his eyes. Joan Lorry, in seat 5C across from Nan, got her buckle open easily, but somehow her ankles were severely twisted, making it impossible for her to stand. She winced in pain as she tried to get up from her seat. Captain Jamison arrived just as she made her second attempt to stand. He grabbed her from behind.

"Please leave me be. I want to die and be with my husband," she said.

Ignoring her, Jamison dragged her backwards down the aisle to the rear exit door. He laid her down at the threshold, jumped down to the grass and lifted her out. He hurried in carrying her from the plane to safety down on the grass. Before she could say another word he was running back to the plane. He returned to help Nan.

"Here I am," he said. "Now let's get this belt open."

He pulled a small knife from his pants pocket, opened the two inch blade and tried to saw Nan's lap belt. The nylon proved extremely hard to cut and after sawing for ten seconds, he had barely cut away any of the thick belt with his somewhat-dull knife.

"Are we going to die?" Nan asked.

"No," replied Jamison as he continued his attempt to cut the belt fabric.

Nan also continued her efforts to get the belt buckle to release, but pushing the button did nothing.

The sirens from the approaching fire trucks were getting louder. Nan glanced out the window and confirmed they were in sight and almost to the plane. She could also see the green grass in the flickering firelight and safety, but Nan knew she was helplessly trapped.

Jamison stopped trying to cut the belt, as it was proving useless, and instead tried to pry at the buckle button. The blade of his pocketknife snapped from his twisting motion and made a loud pinging sound. At that moment Nan looked up into Jamison's eyes. It was the look people have when they know and are resigned to their coming fate. The fate Nan and Jamison were going to share was the sudden end of their lives. Jamison sat down next to Nan. Tears formed in her eyes as she whispered to him, "This is not fair, not fair."

Calm came over her and time seemed to stop. She could no longer hear the fire truck sirens or cries for help. Everything around her was now silent. She turned and looked at Captain

Jamison's face, but it was frozen. Looking about the cabin, she saw nothing moving. Even Stewardess Kimm stood frozen in the aisle like a store mannequin. A glance out the window revealed nothing moving out there, either. Even the rain had stopped. The cabin light didn't flicker, but remained constant. What was going on, she wondered? An epiphany came over her thoughts and somehow she instantly understood that all her future plans, hopes and dreams were infinitely distant, never to be reached. She touched her ring finger and also knew that finding her true love would never happen. Then she began to feel the presence of the other passengers in her thoughts. It was like they were all whispering softly and she could hear each of them, but not quite understand what they were saying; she even heard Captain Jamison's voice, and that of Stewardess Kimm. The voices combined and she could clearly hear them saying in unison,

"Help us, please will someone help us?"

The voices grew stronger and repeated the same words and Nan found herself beginning to chant them over and over along with everyone else. It was as if their minds were all tuned in to each other at that moment. What's happening, she thought? As the repeated words grew ever louder, Nan wondered who would hear them; their voices repeating over and over like a scratched phonograph record. Nan could not make herself stop saying the words. It was as if something had taken over her will at that moment, and even though she could still think clearly, the words continued to repeat,

"Help us, please will someone help us?"

Then all the voices went silent and she stopped repeating the words herself. What was happening? Nan tried the buckle release button again but it wouldn't budge. The light began to flicker again in the cabin and she smelled smoke. Soon the fire truck sirens could be heard, louder and louder in her ears. Help is finally here she thought, but the possibility of more time had already run out.

The fire trucks reached the plane just as the flames reached the remaining gas in the bottom of the fuel truck's tank. The resulting explosion and flames instantly killed Nan, Captain Jamison, Stewardess Kimm, and all other trapped passengers on the plane. Thirteen souls were lost in an instant. The fire crews advanced with their hoses, spraying water and retardant, but the flames proved to be too intense and they were forced to stop in their tracks for a moment. No one still on the plane could have survived the explosion and inferno. The Stapleton Airfield Fire Chief stood with his men, stunned at what he saw, horror etched onto his face by the light of the flickering orange flames.

Huddled together away from the burning plane, the seven saved souls were in shock. Ambulances have arrived and medical teams ran toward them. One member of the medical team approached Joan Lorry where she lay on the ground.

"Lady, are you okay?" he asked.

Joan looked up at him and in a soft voice uttered, "No warning, we had no warning." She repeated her words over and over in the warm, light rain.

PART TWO

Chapter 7 – Stapleton, (Denver) Colorado, May 26, 2007

Moving into his new Denver condo from Chicago, Illinois, Ed Drummond eagerly looked forward to a new chapter in his life. At thirty-five he was an accomplished chemical engineer and quite in demand in the trade. The maestro of the chemical fix was how he saw himself. He occasionally pondered his excellence in his field and always concluded it was just a byproduct of logical reasoning. The money in quickly solving tough industrial chemical problems also paid extremely well. He worked for Chemical Solutions, a nationally renowned, Chicago-based, chemical troubleshooting and consulting company with the best minds in the business and a Fortune 1000 list of clients. They were the first call when a batch of anything chemical went sour on the production floor, or when a company needed professional advice on properly disposing of chemical mishaps. Many of their clients were in the metal plating and electronics businesses and this was Ed's specialty restoring normal operations, day or night, seven days a week. The work was intense at times, but rewarding when he solved the problem and the production managers job was saved. Ed also liked the freedom of project work, as the boring nine-to-five office routine was not for him.

One casualty in his move to Denver revolved around Melinda Duncan; he had left her behind in Chicago, for good. They dated for a long time and lived together in a small downtown apartment for two years, but she chose not to follow Ed to Denver. Their relationship ended after less than two minutes of conversation when he announced that he had been chosen to start up a new Chemical Solutions branch in Denver. Before he could even finish telling her what he thought was wonderful news and the opportunity of a lifetime, she simply said, "I'm not going." Melinda had no desire to relocate with him and restart her nursing career, and that was that.

His new condo on the corner of East 29th Place and Ulster Avenue, in the trendy town of Stapleton had been built on the redeveloped grounds of the former Denver Stapleton Airport after its closing in 1995. Everything about this newly-developed town appealed to him: its close proximity to downtown Denver, the excellent shops and restaurants nearby and the ability to get to the new Denver International Airport in minutes. The fact that everything in the town was new also appealed to him. He enjoyed standing on his condo's rear deck and seeing the old Stapleton Airport control tower looming overhead. Why did they keep it, he often wondered, and what about that old parking garage next to it?

Assisting him in unloading the U-Haul this bright Saturday morning was his new friend, Brian Edmond, an assistant professor in psychology at the University of Denver. They met while Ed was checking out the Denver Wheelers bicycle club two months earlier. Ed was an avid bicyclist and enjoyed the company and camaraderie of those who loved to fly on two wheels; he also enjoyed the exhilaration of the all-out physical effort bicycling entailed. Both considered Lance Armstrong as the man who set the bar for this sport, the endurance king and finder of the holy grail of cycling! Brian was the Wheelers President and when he asked Ed if there was anything he could do for him, little did he know that Ed would take him up on it to help with the move.

After an hour or so the U-Haul was almost empty. Just two bicycles and Ed's prized futon couch remained unloaded.

"Hey Brian," Ed said, "can you help me with the couch?"

Ed was standing inside the U-Haul and he pushed the bulky, oversized futon toward Brian's waiting arms. Wrestling it off the truck and carrying it through the front door went smoothly.

"This is going right in front of the TV," Ed said as they maneuvered the futon into the living room and set it down.

Ed looked at it for a moment and then nudged it several times to its final resting place.

Brian returned with Ed's racing bike, a Big Leg Emma by Dario Pegoretti, and asked where to put it. Ed looked fondly at the sturdy aluminum frame bike.

"Please put Big Emma over there," he said, pointing to the dinning room. "You can leave the trail bike in the truck."

"Then sir, we're done," Brian responded.

"Thanks Brian. How about lunch and a beer on me at Casey's?"

"You're on," Brian replied.

"I'll take the truck back to U-Haul and meet you there in ten minutes," Ed said.

"Sounds like a plan," Brian replied as he waved goodbye and headed to his car.

Chapter 8

Ed locked up the condo and returned the U-Haul to a facility only a mile away, down Quebec Ave. He cycled back to Casey's, his new favorite Irish Pub. Entering the establishment he immediately spotted Brian and slid into the booth.

"Ah, you ordered me a Guinness. What a splendid drink indeed," Ed said, referring to the dark beer with creamy foam sitting in front of him.

Guinness is an acquired taste and Ed had acquired the taste several years earlier on a trip to Dublin, Ireland. They hoisted and touched their glasses and then each enjoyed a sip of heaven.

Lunch turned to talk of tomorrow's monthly Denver Wheelers 100 mile road rally. Brian explained to Ed how the rally was organized and that it would kick off at the Stapleton Town Center. Fifty miles out and back and then a party right here at Casey's. Leave at ten am and everyone's back by three.

Ed was excited about the trek and looked forward to stretching Big Emma's legs.

"Brian," Ed asked, "now exactly what do you teach at DU?"

"It's UD and as little as possible," Brian jokingly replied. "I mean, I'm into a research project that takes up most of my time and effort, but I also lecture three classes in advanced psychology. The project is funded by Uncle Sam and I am really excited about it. We're right on the cutting edge of the science and focused on reading peoples thoughts."

"You've got to be kidding me," Ed said sarcastically.

"Hey, it's not that remote-viewing stuff from the Regan era, not at all," Brian replied. "This project will help brain-injured soldiers communicate to the outside world via their thoughts being read by sophisticated thought-recognition software. We're just getting started on mapping the brain's electrical activity as it relates to words and speech. The software piece of this project is years off, and another California-based team is working on that. Do you remember that old 1982 Clint Eastwood movie *Firefox*? Well, Clint's character is out to steal a Soviet plane whose weapons are controlled by thought recognition in Russian, no less. The gear to do this was in the helmet. Our project is fundamentally like that. Instead of firing the missiles by thought, the brain information would be turned into synthetic speech or text. If we can get just one of those brain injured Iraq war soldiers to talk this way it will be worth it. No more just staring into their eyes and wondering what's going on in there."

Ed nodded his understanding. He was moved to see how committed Brian was to making the project a success.

"And how do you relax?" Ed asked with a smile.

"That's easy. I ride with the Wheelers," Brian replied.

"Hey, that latter part I think I understand," Ed nodded again with a grin.

"And you Ed, what's your story?" questioned Brian.

"I work for Chemical Solutions out of Chicago and I'm starting up an office here in Denver. We've done several big jobs in Colorado and the surrounding states and I accepted the company's offer to set up a new western branch. Besides, I really wanted the change and the challenge. We fix chemical batch problems, advise on cleaning up messes and also consult with companies on environmentally sound ways to dispose of chemical waste and other byproducts from manufacturing processes. Let me put it this way; when your computer breaks down you first try to fix it yourself and then you call technical support. We're the Geek Squad of chemical mess fixing. Doesn't that sound exciting?" They both laughed.

"Let's leave the day jobs behind for now," Ed continued. "Can you give me pointers on the rally tomorrow?"

"You'll love the ride Ed; we're going on the banzai pipeline trek, south toward Colorado Springs on old highway 83 with a turnaround at Crowfoot Creek. There's an old natural gas pipeline beside part of the road that I named the run after."

"Very cute," Ed responded with a nod.

"It's not all uphill or downhill. You get two breaks in each direction and we have two way stations along the way. My wife Sharon will be manning the Crowfoot Creek turnaround station. She'll be ready to wet you down or patch you up. It's really fun."

Ed was getting more excited about the rally the more he heard Brian speak about it. He was also looking forward to meeting new friends and restarting his life. Things were looking up and who knows, Miss Right could be just around the corner.

From what he had seen in Denver so far, he was very optimistic indeed.

They raised and clinked their glasses together one last time to toast the Wheelers.

"Look Brian, I really appreciate the help in unloading the truck. I owe you big time," Ed said.

"Glad I could help a new Wheeler," Brian replied looking at his watch. "Say, I gotta go. Lot's of honey do's at home. See you tomorrow morning. We leave at ten am sharp!"

Then Brian got up, shook hands with Ed and left.

Ed finished his glass of Guinness, paid the check and walked out into the sunshine. He road slowly back to the condo to unpack and organize and wait for the cable guy scheduled to come by at two pm. After the TV and his wireless network were working and getting the condo into pretty good shape, Ed headed off to the supermarket for bachelor refrigerator basics: Lean Cuisines, frozen pizza, prepared salads, snacks, milk, bread, cereal and beer.

Back at the condo with everything put away, it was close to seven pm. Ed sat down on the futon, pushed the remote button and brought his TV to life. He tuned in the Turner Classics channel and stared at the screen, but he wasn't really watching it. His mind was slowly decompressing from the move and the reality that the change he had so wanted in his life had arrived. On a social level, it would all start tomorrow with the Wheelers road rally and meeting new friends who shared a sport he loved. His thoughts turned to Melinda Duncan one last time and what had gone wrong with their relationship. At the beginning she was the 'one' for him and he had thought he was the 'one' in her eyes, but over time that had all faded away.

He fondly remembered being on the futon with Melinda curled up next to him, watching a movie, reading or napping.

Those special moments were all history now. In reviewing their time together he knew when it began and precisely when the relationship finished, but he was not exactly sure when the love had ended. It was the grey area leading up to the end that he was thinking about. Was it one thing or a bunch of things combined that had ended it?

He had his career and business friends and she had hers. Their common interest was cycling. She was very competitive and they enjoyed this part of their relationship immensely, riding through Chicago's Grant Park, as well as all the weekend treks they'd shared. Somehow and somewhere in their time together they went from lovers to friends, the kiss of death to any serious relationship. The moment of truth came when she simply stated, "I'm not going," and Ed did not try to persuade her further. They both had subconsciously made up their minds in advance and were just waiting for this moment to arrive; and when it did, they gave each other 'that look' and the bonds between them broke instantly. At the time, and in Ed's view, Melinda loved Chicago quite clearly more than him, and from Melinda's perspective she thought he loved his job more than her. Somewhere in the middle of those two perspectives was the truth.

Reflecting further on their time together, he finally accepted his share of the blame for the relationship's ultimate failure. His job definitely was a factor, and he did love his work, but he had thought she understood and accepted his crazy hours, his being called out to an assignment in the middle of the night and disappearing for days. Of course, he was sure all the weekends he spent working when they had previously made plans took its toll, too.

Melinda was a nurse and worked long and ever-changing shifts, and weekends as well. It seemed when he was off, she had to work. When they were both off together, it was an exception to the rule. Sometimes they went weeks without seeing each other; their cell phone and e-mail relationships grew stale fast. They passed each other in the bathroom. The word 'drift' came into his mind. Ed concluded they had just drifted apart by circumstances. Living with someone without really living with them was the problem, he thought. They had slid into the role of roommates over time.

Dwelling further on this was no good. Ed realized that none of this could be changed; it was up to him to change his thinking and focus on the future and what was next. Would he ever find the true love of his life? Were his expectations of meeting the real Miss Right way too high? And would he get it right the next time, if that ever occurred? So many questions and so few concrete answers.

"Goodbye Melinda, and Godspeed," Ed said quietly out loud.

Ed had finally cleared his head of her and resolved to put everything behind him. After an hour or so of watching TV the remote dropped from his hand and he fell asleep, exhausted from the move.

Chapter 9

Ed woke on the futon early Sunday morning, greeted by the sun streaming into his condo. He glanced at his watch. Plenty of time to get ready for the road rally. Sitting up he reached over and with the remote, turned off the TV. Day two in paradise, he thought, looking out the living room window. It was going be a warm, sunny spring day. Getting up, he stretched and walked to the kitchen and made a cup of coffee, added some milk to it and proceeded to his bedroom, where it was off with his clothes and into the shower. His thoughts focused on the rally as the warm water and steam brought him fully back to life. He knew the rally would be more challenging than any he had done before and he was curious to see how the 6000 foot altitude would affect him, as well as the Denver area terrain, which was a lot more varied than the flatlands of Illinois. Ed was in excellent physical shape and he tried to build staying fit into his life with cycling.

"Gotta pace yourself on this one Ed," he spoke out loud in the shower.

He also knew the altitude would drain his energy fast, until he got used to it. No going for the gold today, he thought, just nice and easy does it.

After toweling off Ed shaved his day-old beard, dried his brown hair and then began to hunt for his cycling clothes and headgear. Dressed and holding his helmet and shoes he returned to the kitchen for breakfast. Sitting down at the table with a bowl of oatmeal and two slices of whole wheat toast, all buttered with strawberry jam, he thumbed through the roadmap atlas he'd bought for the move and found the Colorado page. He could see Route 83 heading south from Denver and he traced his finger down the page, stopping at Crowfoot Creek.

"Okay, looks like we're going up to 6800 feet today old boy," he muttered. "This should be a good grind."

Big Emma was next on his list. She hadn't had a workout in over a month, and he started by inspecting her from top to bottom. Grips and brakes, campy tire pressure, chain lubed, shifter, seat a-ok. Emma was ready to ride! She was his pride and joy and was custom-built for his 6' 4" height and long legs. The investment was worth it. In the year he'd had Emma she performed flawlessly, always bringing him home. The extra-beefy frame and superb craftsmanship made Big Emma a joy to ride.

Ed finished a whole grain power bar, drank a glass of water, put on his shoes and red helmet and headed to the front door with Big Emma.

"It's show time, Emma," he said out loud.

He cycled to the rally point in front of the Casey's on East 29th Ave. and was greeted by a swarm of multicolored racing jerseys. This was going to be fun. He noticed the lady Wheelers were also participating in the rally and were off to the side in their own smaller group. He estimated that there were over fifty cyclists assembled so far. He coasted to a stop next to one Wheeler and was about to shake hands and introduce himself, when Brian called out his name.

"Hey Ed, glad you're here. We're just about to start." He patted Ed on the back.

Brian held a megaphone in his hand and chatted with Ed for a minute before walking away to the curb. He keyed the megaphone.

"Good morning, ladies and gentlemen, and welcome to the Denver Wheelers second annual banzai pipeline trek."

Those gathered gave a big loud cheer and clapped their hands.

"First I have some announcements. Now, I don't want anyone overdoing it today like last time. We're here to have fun and enjoy the day. Pace yourself and drink your fluids early and often. We have a way station set up at the 25 mile point and at the Crowfoot Creek turnaround point, plus a chase car ready to repair those Schwinn's you're riding," Brian bellowed.

The Wheelers laughed and booed at the same time.

"Seriously, you all have a great, safe trek and come back here hungry and thirsty for a great post-rally party at Casey's. Now we have one of Denver's finest police officers here to provide safe passage until we get out of town. Please give a hand to Officer Rich Ginder."

Everyone clapped as Officer Ginder waved.

"Okay. All riders line up according to your standing behind the squad car. Let the banzai pipeline trek begin!" Brian concluded.

Over 60 cyclists were now assembling two by two behind Officer Ginder's squad car, heading east. His flashing lights led the way out of Stapleton toward Route 83 south. Ed purposely got to the back of the pack, figuring he would move up as the rally progressed.

Ed slowly began to slide into his groove, the controlled tempo that all bikers get into, but he noticed his breathing was heavier due to the altitude. Soon he was moving steadily up the column of riders hugging the right side of the road on their way south to Crowfoot Creek. Brian was absolutely right, it was going to be a challenge going uphill all the way, but the flat spots also came at the right time to conserve his energy. Big Emma also held her own and operated perfectly.

Riding on a two-lane highway was always a little scary, but having the rally Sunday morning meant minimal auto and almost no truck traffic. At twelve-thirty and approaching the Crowfoot Creek turnaround, Ed noticed the first two Wheelers heading back on the opposite side of the road. They appeared to be keeping an exceptionally high pace between them on the downhill side of the run back to Stapleton. Ed continued on and finally came to the turnaround point and got off Emma. Greeting everyone with bottles of water and power bars was a young woman who must have been Sharon Edmond, Brian's wife. She walked over to introduce herself and hand Ed a bottle of water.

"Welcome to the Wheelers. You must be Ed Drummond," she said with a smile and warm handshake. "Brian told me to be on the lookout for a tall stranger," she quipped.

"Thanks Sharon," Ed responded. "It's a pleasure to meet you too! I really appreciate you letting Brian help me move in yesterday. I couldn't have gotten it done without him."

Sharon smiled, handed Ed a bottle of water and asked him if he wanted an energy bar. Ed said yes and she handed him one.

"Here come some more tired and thirsty puppies. I'll see you back at Casey's later and you can tell me all about your move." She stepped away back to her table to grab more water bottles for the inbound bikers.

Ed pushed Big Emma to the side, did some knee bends, finished the power bar, chugged down the water and then refilled his onboard bottle. Soon, Ed mounted back up on Emma, fastened his helmet strap and headed north on 83 for the downhill leg. He felt great as he engaged the gears, slowly bringing Emma up to his pace speed. He figured he was somewhere in the second half of the pack, but more likely near the middle. He was impressed that the Lady Wheelers were just as competitive as the men, as he had been passed by several on the uphill stage.

Ed continued to move up the pack and hoped to finish in the top one-third, if he could hold out. After another hour of hard charging and he figured he was close to the top third. Knowing it was time to hydrate he reached for his water bottle, and seeing a stretch of downhill coasting ahead, he stopped peddling and rose upright, bringing the water bottle up high for a face blast and good drink.

Out of the corner of his eye he saw a car coming onto the pavement right in front of him. Before he could react Ed ran into the back of the Taurus and sailed completely over the top of the car, bouncing on the hood and then somersaulting feet first onto the pavement. His helmet hit the pavement pretty hard. Fortunately, the driver slammed on the brakes and brought the car to a stop, just inches away from running Ed over.

Ed lay there dazed, and felt nothing but his heart racing. He saw people standing over him asking if he was okay, but nothing came out of his mouth in response. Next, he felt hands picking him up and lifting him to the side of the road. Soon the Colorado highway patrol was on the scene along with an ambulance. By that time Ed was coming back to normal, or so he thought. He joked with the paramedics and said he was okay and wanted to finish the race. He tried to stand up slowly to prove his point.

"See, I'm fine," he said, just as his knees buckled and down he went.

The two paramedics caught his fall and lifted him onto the gurney.

"You're going to the emergency room Bub. Your race is over," one of them said.

It took a twenty-minute siren-blaring ambulance ride to reach the hospital emergency entrance. Ed continued to say that he didn't want any treatment and insisted on walking into the ER.

"Look Bub, you're staying on that gurney until the ER doc says you can get up," the paramedic said.

They unloaded him from the ambulance and wheeled him into the emergency room at the new Stapleton General Hospital. The ER orderlies transferred Ed to a hospital cart and soon the ER triage nurse was looking down at him. She took his vitals and asked if he was dizzy or nauseous. Ed replied no. She made notes on the clipboard and said the ER doctor would be right with him. Ed knew he had taken a hard crash, the worst of his biking experience.

"Hi, I'm Doctor Holder," she said, looking down at Ed. "I see you took a pretty nasty fall. That helmet probably saved your life. To be on the safe side I'm ordering a MRI for you to be sure nothing's broken in there. Now remember, Mr. Drummond, head injuries take 24 to 48 hours to fully manifest themselves. During that time you may be dizzy, nauseous, and weak. You've got to take it easy and rest at home."

Ed nodded his concurrence and a moment later he was being wheeled by an orderly to the MRI imaging department. When he was finished they brought him back to the ER waiting room. After waiting around an hour or so, Dr. Holder came out to tell him that his brain scan looked great, with no internal damage they could see.

"Ed, you are one lucky man," the doctor said. "You have a scrapped arm and leg, and nothing broken. You're going to be okay, but you must go home now and rest. Just take two Advil if you get a headache. We've made a follow-up appointment for you next week with our hospital neurosurgeon. The nurse will give you the date and time with your paperwork." An orderly appeared with a wheel chair and his paperwork and helped Ed first to sit up on the gurney and then helped him to stand for a moment before settling Ed into the wheelchair.

"Sorry sir, hospital rules require that we wheel you out to your ride home. And sir, your friends are waiting for you," the orderly said.

As Ed entered the waiting room he saw Brian and Sharon Edmond sitting next to the door.

"Hi guys," Ed said rather sheepishly. "Thanks for coming by."

"Boy Ed, sorry about you spill. I heard that guy pulled right out in front of you," Brian said.

"Man, bad move on my part. I was coasting and getting a drink and took my eyes off the road for just an instant and then bam, everything went into slow motion. The good news is that the doc says I'm okay, except for these scrapes," Ed said, pointing to his left arm and leg bandages.

"Welcome to Denver. Now let's get you home," Brian responded.

The orderly wheeled Ed to the outside entrance and waited for Brian to return with his car. Ed slid into front seat, and with Sharon in the back they headed for Ed's condo. Arriving, they helped him inside and onto his futon.

Ed asked about Big Emma and Brian told him not to worry, that she was outside on his bike rack and he would bring her in shortly.

"She's got a bent front wheel, a broken pedal and a few scrapes here and there, but nothing that can't be fixed. She'll live to ride again, just like you!" Brian quipped.

"Want anything to eat or drink?" Sharon asked.

"No, thanks," was Ed's first response. "I'll just lie here on the couch for a while and rest." He paused. "On second thought, I could use a glass of water and that bottle of Advil in my medicine cabinet."

Soon a large glass of ice water and the Advil were placed in front of him on the coffee table. After a few minutes discussing his accident and the trek, Brian and Sharon said goodbye and wished him well.

"Take care of yourself and call me tomorrow," Brian said as he closed the door behind Sharon on their way out.

Ed lay motionless with his head propped up on a pillow for ten minutes or so before reaching for the Advil and water. In another ten minutes he stiffly got up and walked even slower to his bedroom, where he took off his cycling gear and headed for his second hot shower of the day. After drying off he put on his dark blue Chicago Bears sweat shirt and pants. For some reason, he reached for his favorite Bay Rum aftershave lotion on the dresser and splashed some on his face. He also grabbed his travel alarm clock from the dresser and set the time for six am, then headed back to the living room. Ed turned on the TV with the remote and settled back down on the futon.

"What a day, what a day indeed," he mumbled. "Day two in Denver and I almost get killed. What's next?"

The hot shower and Advil made him very comfortable and masked the aches and pains of the fall. Ed started to watch a movie, but soon his eyes closed and he nodded off.

Chapter 10

Ed woke and found himself seated in what appeared to be a small closet illuminated by two wall lights. Looking around further he saw that it looked a lot like an airplane lavatory, but nothing resembling the jets he's traveled on. It felt like he was sitting on a toilet, and a quick look down confirmed it. He then noticed the noise and felt the vibration of engines, but these were not the sounds or feelings of a jet. He looked at the small aluminum sink staring him in the face and then glanced at the white cloth towels folded neatly on the adjacent counter; they were embroidered with the United Airlines emblem.

This can't be real, he said to himself. I must be dreaming. Rising slowly he looked at his face in the mirror. He was still wearing his Bear's sweats. Ed grasped the door handle, pushed the lever down and slowly opened the door. He stepped out of the lavatory and looked into a plane cabin he didn't recognize. What kind of plane is this, and where am I? This has got to be a dream.

He took another step and saw an aisle with two seats on the left side and one on the right. People were reading, talking, and looking out the windows. It was still daylight outside and the sun shone in to fully illuminate the cabin. Just then, a woman in a blue suit with golden wings on her coat walked down the aisle and approached him.

"Where did you come from?" she asked with an inquisitive look.

"In there," Ed replied, pointing back to the lavatory. "In there."

"Listen mister, did you get on in Omaha?" she asked.

"No ma'am, I just came from in there," he repeated, pointing again to the lavatory.

"You must be a stowaway, then," she said. "And what is your name, sir?"

"I'm Ed Drummond and I live in Denver," Ed replies.

"Well, that's where this flight is headed, Mr. Drummond. Please come with me," she said as she turned and started to walk up the aisle. Ed followed until she stopped at the first vacant seat on the left.

"Please sit down here while I notify the captain," she said.

Ed nodded and sat down in the seat. It was soft, like an easy chair, with plenty of legroom. He turned his head slowly to his left, toward the woman passenger in the window seat. Her head was turning from looking out the window to see who had just sat down next to her. Their eyes met. Ed didn't know what to say and kept looking at her face. How awkward, he thought, and finally the woman extended her right hand.

"Hello, I'm Nan Orland," she said. "I don't think I noticed you before."

Ed extended his hand to grasp hers, which was curious, as the women he's known don't shake hands much. He gently squeezed and shook her hand.

"I'm Ed Drummond from Denver, Colorado," he said.

"Well that makes two of us, Mr. Drummond," she replied, smiling brightly. Ed instantly smiled back. He let go of her hand but could not turn away from her face. He continued his gaze for another moment. Nan told him the captain had just announced that they were about an hour from landing at Stapleton Airfield. Ed thought that curious, since Stapleton had been closed for over ten years.

"You mean Denver International don't you?" Ed asked.

"No, where is that?" she said.

Ed began to realize something wasn't quite right. Was this a dream after all?

"Oh, Denver International is what I hear they're going to call Stapleton Airfield in the future," he replied. "Miss Orland, what kind of plane is this?"

"Why, this is a brand new Super DC-3. My daddy says it's more powerful and comfortable than the older version, but I wouldn't know, as this is my first airplane ride," she said.

"Miss Orland, can you tell me what today's date is?"

"First, please call me Nan. Today is May 23, 1952," she replied.

Ed slowly turned forward and leaned his head back against the seat. His mind raced, not fully believing what he had heard. He'd never had a dream like this before, but was it a dream? Ed wasn't sure, but he was now intrigued with the situation and was definitely attracted to his seatmate. She was the most initially captivating and beautiful woman he had ever met, and dream or not, he wanted to get to know her better.

Coming down the aisle was a man in a blue suit with wings on his chest, gold braid on his hat and hash marks on his coat cuffs. He stopped at Ed's seat.

"I'm Captain Jamison. Would you please step to the rear of the plane for a moment?" he asked.

Ed got up from his seat. Now the other passengers were looking at him. He walked to the back of the plane.

"Mr. Drummond, Stewardess Kimm informs me you are a stowaway. Is that so?" Jamison asked pointedly.

"Not exactly, sir. I don't know how I got on this plane or why I'm here. My first recollection was walking out from the lavatory over there," he said, pointing to the lavatory door. "I think this is a dream I'm having and I'll wake up soon."

Captain Jamison looked at Stewardess Kimm with a 'we have a mental case on board' look.

"When we land in Denver, I'm going to turn you over to the authorities. It will be up to them to decide what to do. Please return to your seat. We'll be landing in less than an hour," Jamison said.

"I mean you no harm, I truly don't know how I got here," Ed replied.

With that, the captain turned and walked up the aisle, returning to the cockpit. Stewardess Kimm followed Ed back to seat 5B. A few of the passengers looked at Ed, but most continued with what they were doing. As Ed sat down, Nan, curious as to what was going on, asked Ed, "Mind explaining what all that was about?"

Ed turned in his seat to face her.

"Nan, I don't know how I got on this plane, or why I'm here. I think this is a dream and that nothing here is real, that you're not real."

Nan now smiled and laughed. Ed, realizing how strange this must sound to her, began to laugh too.

"Tell me where you think you came from," Nan questioned.

"For starters, I just moved to Denver from Chicago. I'm a chemical engineer. This morning was Sunday, May 27, 2007. I got up and went on a bicycle road rally with the Denver Wheelers Bicycle Club and close to the end of the race I had an accident and was taken to the hospital. I went home and lay down on my couch and the next thing I remember is waking up sitting on the toilet in the lavatory of this plane," Ed said, matter-of-factly.

Nan looked at him skeptically, but on some unknown level she seemed to believe him.

"Ed, if what you say is true, how can you prove it?" Nan asked.

Ed looked down at his sweat pants and knew he had no identification on him, nothing.

"I guess you'll just have to believe me that I'm telling the truth," he said.

Then, as he put both hands on his cheeks, he remembered the Bay Rum aftershave he'd splashed on his face. He turned to Nan and told her that he had put on some aftershave – could she smell it? Nan leaned over near his face and nodded that she could smell his aftershave.

"Why, that's Bay Rum. My father wears it all the time," she said.

Ed realized that proved nothing. If it was his dream and he was imagining her, of course she would know what aftershave he was wearing. But she should also know everything about him as well; everyone in this dream, he thought, would know all about him.

"I don't know what's going on here, but if I'm imagining you I'm glad we have met, dream, reality or whatever," Ed said.

Nan blushed, as no one had ever said that to her before.

"Okay, let's each start from the beginning. Can you tell me about Nan?' he asked.

Just then Captain Jamison came on the address system.

"Ladies and gentlemen, we'll be landing in Denver in about thirty minutes and I'll have you at the terminal at six pm. Denver control says we're just ahead of a big thunder storm, with gusty winds, so we may have a few bumps along the way. Please return to your seats and fasten your seatbelts."

Ed calculated he had been on the plane just over half an hour. It was turning into a wonderful dream, one like he had never experienced. Everything was so lifelike, so real: the rich detail of the airplane, the intriguing woman sitting next to him, everything. He could see the individual strands of her brown hair. He was trying to remember every detail, especially everything about her, she who he was strongly attracted to for some unknown reason. Is it possible, he thought, to meet the girl of your dreams in a dream?

Ed looked out the window and it was still daylight. He buckled his seatbelt and so did Nan. The plane rolled to the right and shuddered slightly in what Ed guessed was the approaching storm front.

"Guess we're in for a bumpy ride," Ed said.

"Oh, my horse can buck better than this," Nan replied. "I live on a ranch just outside Denver. My family owns the Orland Cattle Company. Ever heard of us in the future, Ed?" she jokingly asked.

"No, I haven't." Ed shook his head.

They bantered back and forth, not paying attention to the plane's bumpy ride, just to each other. Ed was convinced that this was all a dream, but the most fantastic dream he had ever experienced. He had no idea what a Super DC-3 was, had never been on one, or any DC-3, for that matter. Whose dream was this anyway? Was this just his dream, or could it be Nan's, or was it a shared dream or reality experience? Ed's mind continued to race. The questions now came to him faster and faster, but without answers. He asked Nan question after question about her brothers, parents, the Orland Cattle Company, what she was doing in Chicago, where she went to school, how she got on this flight, everything. She asked him what life was like in 2007. When he told her that the US was at war in Iraq and Afghanistan, she laughed.

Chapter 11

Ed heard and felt the landing gear go down.

"We're very close to Denver Inter ... err, Stapleton Airfield," Ed said to Nan, catching himself.

He glanced down at Nan's wristwatch and saw it was close to six pm. The plane suddenly pitched up, giving Ed that funny roller coaster feeling in his stomach, and he knew something was wrong. Nan reached over and grabbed Ed's hand. He held her tight as his stomach turned again to let him know he was heading down fast. In the next moment the plane struck the runway then bounced into the air and hit the ground again. Both were tossed around in their seats. He asked her if she was okay. She responded that she was fine, just shaken and a bit dazed, but it was no worse than being thrown from her horse. He leaned forward and looked out the left window and saw that they were still rocketing down the runway, accompanied by a very loud crunching and grinding sound with a stream of trailing sparks. He could see the engines had stopped and felt the plane slowly turning until, still looking out the left window, Ed realized he was looking back down the runway. He held Nan as close as he could. He saw the bright field landing lights and soon the control tower and rotating beacon passed by. The rain was also coming down pretty hard.

"Is this thing ever going to stop?" he said to Nan

Just then another big jolt pushed Nan closer against him. She was fully awake, but Ed thought she might be in a state of shock. They must have hit something to slow them, but no, they were still moving and then in the next moment the plane stopped. Outside appeared bright as daylight. Ed looked back out the window and saw the trail of flames behind the plane growing closer and he knew the entire plane would be on fire in an instant.

The other passengers around them began screaming and yelling for help. Glancing up the cabin, Ed noticed that some were unconscious in their seats. He spied Captain Jamison trying to help passengers in the front of the cabin.

"Nan, let's get the hell out here," he said.

Ed pushed the button on his seatbelt and it instantly released. Nan, slightly dazed, but coming back to her full senses, asked Ed what was happening.

"We've been in an accident and we need to get out of here," he said.

Nan pushed the button on her seatbelt buckle but it wouldn't release. Ed reached over and pushed the button, then tugged on the belt, with the same result.

"We need some help here, captain," Ed shouted as Captain Jamison walked down the aisle carrying an unconscious man to the exit door and safety.

"Right back," he responded over his shoulder.

Stewardess Kimm then raced up the aisle, past Ed to the passengers in the front cabin. In a moment Captain Jamison returned, but he grabbed the women across the aisle from them in seat 5C who was attempting to get up and was obviously in excruciating pain. The captain grabbed her from behind and dragged her backwards down the aisle toward the exit door and out of Ed's sight. Ed thought he heard her say something about wanting to die, but his focus returned to Nan. Ed continued to push the button on the buckle and tug at the seatbelt trying to free her. Nan was beginning to panic.

"Here I am," Captain Jamison shouted as he returned, motioning for Ed to get up and out of his seat. "That another locked buckle I see?"

Standing in the aisle, and looking at Nan, Ed could see Jamison pull a small knife from his pocket and begin to saw Nan's seatbelt. He heard her ask Jamison if they were going to die and heard his simple response: "No." Ed smelled smoke filling the top of the cabin and heard the sirens outside getting closer.

Seeing that Jamison was getting nowhere in cutting the belt, Ed focused on freeing Nan – but how? Maybe a dinner knife, or spoon pried into the buckle would release the mechanism. He turned around and began to run up the aisle toward the galley, but then a loud buzzing sound filled his ears. Louder and louder … buzz, buzz, buzz … it would not stop ringing in his ears. What was that BUZZING? Ed saw a bright orange flash of light and felt heat like an oven burning his face, and then silence and darkness.

Chapter 12

Ed woke up standing next to the futon in his living room with beads of perspiration clinging to his forehead. His travel alarm was buzzing on the coffee table, and its irritating buzz-buzz-buzz sound. He reached down and shut the alarm off and sat back down on the futon. The early morning sun was just peeking through the window. It was now six on Monday morning.

"Wow, did I have a dream or what?" Ed said out loud.

It was the most exhilarating dream he had ever experienced. So real, so lifelike, so fresh in his mind that he remembered it all, even a beautiful woman named Nan Orland – especially Nan. This is all so crazy, he thought, I've never had such an intense dream like that before. I talked to those people, I could smell Nan's perfume, and I could smell the smoke, feel the heat. She could smell my aftershave and even knew the brand name. How was all this possible? After thinking further he dismissed everything as his mind and vivid imagination assembling the entire dream sequence. However, he had unanswered questions about the experience. Did his accident have anything to do with this? His subconscious mind would not let this drop without answers; after all, his job was to solve problems and surely this was a problem his mind needed to resolve. Could any of it be real, or was it one hundred percent dream?

Ed stood up and began to think about work, but he remembered his accident and the doctor's orders to take it easy for two days.

"Okay. Doc wins," he said out loud and headed for the shower.

He was a bit sore, especially his neck and the two big road rash spots on his left leg and arm. A hot shower would do wonders to loosen him up. Deciding to work from the condo for the day, at eight am he called Teeah, the new office secretary he had hired on a previous visit to Denver, to tell her that he would be working from home and to forward all calls to his cell phone.

Ed fired up his laptop on the kitchen table, found his wireless network for the Internet and logged on to the company's remote gateway. He handled a dozen e-mails, returned several calls, and made one appointment for Thursday, but thoughts of his dream drifted in and out of his work all morning, interfering with his concentration.

"Okay Drummond, let's get this over with and prove to yourself once and for all that none of it ever happened," he said out loud.

He brought up the Internet search engine Google on his laptop and entered 'Stapleton Airfield accidents.' To his amazement a list of accidents appeared, going back to the 1940s. Ed scanned the list and stopped at the date May 23, 1952. It read that

United Airlines flight 77, a DC-3, crash-landed in a storm with thirteen dead.

"So there was an accident," Ed said out loud in a raised voice, stunned at the revelation.

He typed 'May 23, 1952 Stapleton airplane accident' into Google and hit the search button. At the top of the search list was a National Oceanic and Atmospheric Administration Microburst Handbook page, which had the following entry:

> ...Earlier, a court investigating a wind-shear-related accident at Denver's Stapleton Airfield that happened 23 May 1952 during a thunderstorm, concluded that 'the accident was the result of a loss of height and air speed caused by the aircraft encountering, at approximately 100 ft during landing, an unpredictable thunderstorm cell which gave rise to a sudden downdraft of wind. This ruling, perhaps because of its tentative wording, does not seem to have alerted the rest of the aviation world to the dangers of thunderstorm downdrafts to landing aircraft...

Ed could not believe what he was reading. How could he have dreamt about something he never knew happened, and in 1952, no less?

He typed 'Nan Orland Denver' into Google, but nothing came back. But the archives at *The Denver Post* would surely have something on this accident. It was worth a try, he said to himself, as he picked up his cell phone and called the paper's information desk. A woman answered. He asked about issues of the paper from 1952. She laughed and said that they were on microfiche in the basement reference room of the main Denver Public Library. Ed thanked her and closed his cell phone.

Ed looked up the library's address online and wrote it down. He had to run some errands anyway, and a quick look at those old archives wouldn't hurt. He piled into his Explorer and drove downtown.

At the library Ed went to the reference room in the basement and asked the attendant for the microfiche for the May 24, 1952, issue of *The Denver Post.* She handed him a small box.

"These are all issues of the Post for May through September 1952," she said.

Ed thanked her and walked over to one of the old microfiche readers, sat down and loaded the fiche for the week he wanted. Scrolling, he brought on the screen the front-page headline for May 24, 1952:

13 DEAD IN FATAL STAPLETON

AIRFIELD CRASH – 7 SURVIVE

There was a picture of the DC-3 plane on fire, with firemen hosing it down. Continuing down the first page headline column he read:

> Stapleton Airfield – United Airlines flight 77 from Chicago crashed and burned last night at approximately six pm while landing during a thunderstorm. Thirteen passengers and crew died in the fiery crash. Miraculously, seven passengers survived. Exact cause of the accident is under investigation by the FAA. John Bourke, who is heading the investigation, stated that pilot Eric Jamison and co-pilot Mark Palmer were veteran United Airline pilots with over 35 years of experience between them. The wreckage would be moved to a hanger for detail examination. Notable in those killed in the crash were Denver attorney Scott Rockwell and his wife, Eloise, and Miss Nan Orland, daughter of Cattle magnate Paul Orland…

Ed stopped reading further when his eyes saw the name Nan Orland and slowly pushed back his chair. How could he dream about things he knew nothing about – an airplane crash that really happened fifty-five years ago? And talking with some of those people, especially Nan Orland? How was this possible? Leaning forward, he continued to read the story:

> … One survivor willing to comment stated the crew was heroic in getting passengers out of the plane and thought that everyone had time to get out. The plane, a new Super DC-3, had only been in service four months and had all the latest radio and navigation aids. Eyewitnesses said the plane appeared to fall flat onto the runway before beginning a long skid. The sturdy DC-3 survived the crash from the air to the ground only to ram into a fuel truck, which ultimately exploded, killing all remaining onboard. A team of aircraft engineers from the Douglas Aircraft factory in Santa Monica, California, is en route to the scene to study the accident and tragic loss of life. All airport traffic was suspended until early this morning. Those that perished in the crash are …

Ed pushed back again. He felt that now that he was a survivor of the crash himself and could corroborate the facts, he agreed everyone could have gotten out if only those seatbelt buckles had opened.

"What am I saying?" Ed muttered, hitting the page print button on the machine.

He moved to the obituary page and was greeted by Nan's smiling picture in the upper left column. Stunned at seeing her face, he was totally confused at how he could know exactly what she looked like.

"It was her face. I met her in my dream," Ed whispered.

Ed stared at her picture for the longest time. "It's her, it's her," he repeated over and over. "I would know those eyes anywhere. What beautiful eyes."

For the first time in his adult life Ed felt like he was losing it … maybe freaking-out was the operative word. No way can this be happening. It was her face, her hair, her smile. He continued to read:

> Nan Orland Dies in Plane Crash
>
> *(Picture)*
>
> Miss Orland, age 26, of Denver, Colorado, died tragically yesterday in the United Airlines plane crash at Stapleton Airfield. She was returning home from a business trip to Chicago, where she and her father attended the Chicago International Stockman's Exposition and at which their prize bull, Topper, won best of show. Nan was a vice president and business manager for the family's business, the Orland Cattle Company. Nan graduated from the University of Denver in 1947 with a degree in business administration. She is survived by her father and mother, Paul and Ellie Orland, and younger brother Avery Orland. Her older brother, Ken Orland, was killed in World War II action in Normandy just days after the D-Day invasion. Services and internment will be at Oaklawn Memorial Park ….

Ed hit the page print button again. He moved the fiche forward to the May 25, 1952, edition. On the front page:

AIRPLANE CRASH VICTIMS LOCKED

INTO THEIR SEATS

> Stapleton Airfield – Investigators revealed that all ten passengers who died were still belted into their seats when the plane exploded. Rescuers had to cut through the seatbelts to remove the bodies. John Bourke, FAA chief investigator, said it appeared all passengers could have escaped if the seatbelt buckles had released. He said that the Airline crew was doing everything they could to free all the passengers at the time of the explosion, heroically losing their lives in the attempt. Further investigation will determine the exact cause of the apparent seatbelt failure...

Ed hit the page print button again. Switching off the microfiche machine, he gathered his copies, returned the box of microfiche to the attendant, and walked out of the library into the bright sun. He climbed into his Explorer, put the key into the ignition, but did not start the motor. He had just confirmed almost every fact of the previous night's dream. Is it coincidence that he already knew everything he read on the microfiche? While pondering what to do next, his cell phone rang – chirp, chirp, chirp. It was Brian Edmond checking up on him.

"Brian, I'm glad you called. I wanted to talk to you too," Ed spoke into his cell phone.

"How are you doing?" Brian asked.

"Well, physically I'm okay. Hurting a bit, but nothing I won't get over. Say, Brian, can we meet at Casey's later this afternoon, or this evening? I really need to go over a few things with you," Ed asked him.

"Sure, how does five-thirty sound?" Brian replied. "It's on my way home."

"That's great, Brian. See you then. Goodbye." Ed closed his cell phone. He turned the key in the ignition and drove home to his Stapleton condo.

Chapter 13

Ed got to Casey's just before five-thirty and was seated in a booth with a window overlooking Quebec Avenue. He stared out at the rush hour traffic driving by and then glanced over to the door.

"Hey Brian, over here," Ed called out and waved.

Brian walked over and sat down. The waitress followed just behind him.

"Hello boys, what'll ya have?" she asked.

Brian ordered a Coors light and Ed his beloved glass of Guinness.

"Say, you don't look too bad for an accident victim," Brian said with a smile.

"As I said on the phone, I'm physically okay. The cuts and bruises will all heal, but I had this dream last night. The most intense and realistic dream I have ever had, and, get this, the dream turned out to be true. I met and talked with a beautiful woman who totally captivated me," Ed started.

"Ed, it's probably a result of your head injury. You've somehow unlocked a treasure trove of memories we all record from day one, and can't always get at. Meeting the girl of your dreams in a dream is normal. It's what you're searching for right now, my friend, isn't it?" Brian said with a smile.

The waitress returned with their drinks and placed each glass on a Casey's cloverleaf coaster.

"I believe you, except that I never knew anything about the facts of this dream before I dreamt them. It was a plane crash in 1952 that occurred right here in Stapleton. I mean, right here, at the old Stapleton Airfield, and I think really near where my condo is. Look, I made copies of the newspaper from May 24, 1952, that reported the crash. Here, look at these newspaper clippings for yourself." He handed them to Brian, who glanced at each page.

"And this is the woman you met in your dream?" Brian asked, pointing to the picture of Nan Orland.

Ed nodded.

"Well, you have extremely good taste Ed," Brian said.

He paused and continued to look at the pages, thought for a moment, put the pages down slowly and looked into Ed's eyes.

"My friend, you had a very serious accident yesterday, and thank God you're okay. It's very normal to have realistic dreams and there doesn't have to be an explanation or reason – they just happen. I think all this was conjured up by your subconscious mind. Was this a coincidence? Maybe it was. Somehow, you knew something about this plane crash, or any plane crash. And remember, you've been recording stuff in your brain for thirty-five years, consciously and unconsciously." Brian spoke in a reassuring tone.

Ed smiled, nodded again and lifted his glass to take a sip.

"You're right Brian, it was only a dream. I made it up and I guess I just won the dream lottery," he said.

"Take it easy, friend. The odds of repeating the same dream, unless there's sex involved, of course, is a million to one. Maybe you've got some good book material here, Ed," Brian replied jokingly.

With that comment they both laughed out loud, which broke all the tension Ed had built up during the day. He signaled the waitress over to order dinner.

"Sorry Ed, but I have to go home. Sharon will kill me if I come home fed and she has dinner waiting. I'll take a rain check," Brian said as he handed back Ed's newspaper copies.

Standing, he shook Ed's hand and departed. Ed decided to leave too and asked the waitress for the check. Neither had finished their drink. Leaving cash on the table, Ed got up, left Casey's and drove back to his condo, mentally exhausted.

He parked in the garage, headed inside and changed into the same Chicago Bears sweats, then headed to the kitchen for something to eat. He pulled a frozen pizza from the freezer and turned on the oven. Ed poured himself a glass of ice water and took an Advil. While waiting for the oven to heat up, he plopped down on the futon and switched on the TV. He stopped at the Turner Classic Movie channel again. It was playing the Christopher Reeves and Jane Seymour movie *Somewhere In Time,* the cult classic time travel romance with the funny 'meet your love in heaven after death' ending. Still, he liked the story and characters.

"At least they loved each other across time, even if it could never be," Ed said to himself. He believed that time travel of any kind was impossible. It just wasn't logical, but it made for great stories and he loved all stories dealing with time.

Just then the oven beeped, signaling it was ready. Ed walked to the kitchen and put the pizza in the oven, grabbed the portable timer and set it for fifty-five minutes. He brought it with him back to the futon, where he stretched out and continued to watch the movie. The days' activity, especially the mental stress, had really made him tired; however, he tried to remain alert and awake by staring at the movie on the big screen. After ten minutes of struggling to stay awake, Ed blinked and the screen projected a picture of a small room. The noise of droning piston aircraft engines filled his living room from the wireless surround sound speakers. Ed sat up; the picture on the screen was exactly what he had seen while sitting on the toilet in the DC-3 lavatory of his dream. How did this get on the screen? Something awfully funny was going on here. Perhaps he had seen his dream in a movie and it was just playing back, or perhaps the cable guy left a test DVD in the player, but this was weird. Ed stood up and hit his head on something metallic, which caused his eyes to instinctively close for a moment.

"Ouch, that hurt." He raised his hand to his head and rubbed it.

"What the hell is going on here?" he said, in total disbelief as he opened his eyes.

Chapter 14

Ed found himself hunched over, holding his head and staring once again into the lavatory mirror of the Super DC-3. He was still wearing his Chicago Bears sweat suit. This can't be happening, he said to himself. Dreams don't repeat like this; well, that's what Brian said, anyway. Ed continued to rub his head, and then pinched himself hard on the arm to see if he would wake up. The drone of the plane's engines filled his ears, as before.

He fully remembered everything about his dream; his trip to the library that afternoon and Brian's comments at Casey's a couple of hours ago that the odds were a million to one a dream would repeat. His hand reached for the door lever, but he pulled back and sat down on the toilet seat to think.

"Okay Drummond, you're in the dream again, now what?" he mumbled out loud.

He wondered if he could change anything in this dream experience from before and figured he had nothing to lose. If the dream turned out to be reality, then maybe he could alter the outcome; he became determined to see if he could change things. Now he knew the outcome of the first dream, he knew some of the passengers and crew and he knew Nan, just outside the door in seat 5A. Ed immediately came up with a plan. He would tell the captain to divert the plane to another airport as it was going to crash. Then he could save everyone onboard. He'd wake up, Google the crash and it wouldn't be there. Ed stood and looked into the mirror again.

"Let's see if we can change any of this for the good," he said as he slowly opened the lavatory door and stepped out into the cabin.

Just as before, Stewardess Kimm noticed him and walked down the aisle, right up to him.

"Where did you come from?" she asked with the same inquisitive look on her face.

"In there," Ed replied, pointing back to the lavatory. "In there."

"Listen mister, did you get on in Omaha?" she asked.

"No ma'am, I just came from in there," he repeated, pointing again to the lavatory.

"You must be a stowaway then," she said. "And what is your name, sir?"

"Miss Kimm, my name is Ed Drummond and I live in Denver. I want to talk with Captain Jamison right away. I've something very important to tell him. It's a matter of life or death," Ed replied.

Stewardess Kimm looked at him curiously.

"Please come with me," she said.

He followed her up the aisle, looking at the back of Nan's head. The stewardess stopped at Nan's seat and turned around.

"Please sit down here while I notify the captain," she said.

Ed nodded and sat down in the seat next to Nan. Was he having a case of déjà vu, or what? Ed felt confident that he could change things. He already had; the dialogue with Stewardess Kimm had changed, but he was now seated next to Nan and wanted to try and remember exactly what he said and did in the first dream. Her head turned towards him and their eyes met again, just like the first time, and Ed still didn't know what to say. He was totally mesmerized by her. Words would not come out of his mouth. She extended her hand again and introduced herself, just like before.

"Hello, I'm Nan Orland. I don't think I noticed you before," she said.

He reached over, clasped her hand and gently shook it.

"I'm Ed Drummond from Denver, Colorado," he said.

"Well that makes two of us, Mr. Drummond," she replied, smiling brightly. Ed smiled back.

This time he forgot to let her hand go and continued to hold it. Noticing his error, he let go, but continued to look at her face. He had grown to admire her face and was sure they were meant for each other, as crazy as it all seemed. When his stare became uncomfortably obvious he began to tell her how he got on the plane.

"May I call you Nan?" he asked.

"Of course," she replied.

"Nan, I'm from the future. The year 2007, to be exact," he said.

Before he could finish his sentence, someone tapped him on the shoulder. Turning slowly in his seat towards the aisle, Ed looked up to see Captain Jamison and Stewardess Kimm looking down at him.

"I'm Captain Jamison. Would you please step to the rear of the plane for a moment?" he strongly commanded.

Ed got up from his seat and walked down the aisle to the back of the plane. Jamison and Kimm looked at him.

"Mr. Drummond, Stewardess Kimm informs me you are a stowaway. Is that so?" he asked.

"No sir, I'm not. This may be hard for you to believe, but I'm having a dream and am here to warn you that this plane will crash on landing in Denver, during a severe thunderstorm caused by a wind shear effect. The forceful downdraft will push the plane down onto the runway, hard. You can't recover from the downdraft. Ten passengers and all the crew, including yourself and Stewardess Kimm, will die if you don't divert now to another airport."

Captain Jamison looked at Stewardess Kimm to confirm that they had a mental case on board. In such circumstances, he had been trained to calmly agree with non-violent passengers. Since they would be on the ground in less than an hour, he thought it best to play along and let the Denver authorities handle the man.

"Mr. Drummond, I no doubt believe you want to save my plane and passengers from harm. I will call Denver control and verify the severe weather conditions you predict and will take your diversion request under advisement with United's Operation Center in Chicago. Is that fair?" Jamison intoned.

Ed responded that yes, it would be the thing to do. Jamison asked Ed to return to his seat and that he would get right back to Ed after his radio calls. Captain Jamison returned to the cockpit and Ed sat down again next to Nan. He turned towards her.

"Mind explaining what all that was about Mr. Drummond," she asked.

"Nan, I don't know how I got on this plane, or why I'm here. I think this is a dream, but it's a real dream, and it could be your dream for all I know," Ed said.

Nan now smiled and laughed. Ed again realized how strange this must sound to her and also began to laugh.

"Tell me again where you think you came from," Nan questioned.

Ed repeated his reply from the first dream, that he was a chemical engineer and had just moved to Denver from Chicago. He told her again he was from the future and that after his bicycle accident this past Sunday, May 27, 2007, he fell asleep in his condo and woke up on the plane. He told her that they met in his first dream, and that he knew all about her, her family and job, but he stopped short before revealing he knew that she would die in the crash landing.

"May I call you Ed?" she asked.

"Yes," he replied.

"Ed, you seem well informed about me, but it's nothing that hasn't been in the Denver newspaper before," she said.

"Well, I know your prize bull named Topper just won best of show in Chicago," Ed said.

Nan paused, looked intently at Ed's eyes and face, and felt something she had never felt before. It ran deep. What is it about this man that makes me so comfortable and at ease?

Ed next said something that startled Nan.

"Nan, I am here to save you and everyone on this plane from a horrible crash landing at Stapleton Airfield. I told Captain Jamison that he must divert this plane to another airfield until the storm in Denver passes. You'll get home late, but alive."

"What do you mean by save me?" she asked.

"In my dream, and in reality, this plane crashes on landing and you die trapped in your seat," he said.

Nan looked at him, expressionless for a moment, and then a smile came back to her face.

"You paint a very bleak picture Ed," she said, still listening intently. "How did you escape from the first crash you dreamed? And if you were here before, why didn't you save me and everyone then?"

"Nan, I didn't know the plane was going to crash in my first dream and I didn't know what caused your death until it was too late. The plane exploded and I woke up. It was your seatbelt that kept you from escaping the crash. Yours is defective and wouldn't unlock. I tried to free you, God knows I tried, and Captain Jamison tried too, but time ran out for all of us. Look Nan, if Captain Jamison just lands the plane now, you'll be delayed in getting to Denver, but you'll have a wonderful life, I'm sure of it. The plane cannot land as planned or you will perish, and many of the other passengers will die as well. It's as simple as that," Ed told her.

Just then Captain Jamison came down the aisle; he looked at Ed and pointed to the back of the plane. Ed turned to Nan, and told her not to worry, he'd be right back. He stood up and walked to the back of the plane.

"I've called Denver control. They confirm a thunderstorm is approaching, but is not expected until after we land. It's dry as a bone at the field now. Chicago confirms the weather forecast and will not authorize a diversion. This plane will land safely in Denver and on time. Mr. Drummond, we'll go over your prophecy and flight theories on the ground. I'm sorry, but I must follow my orders," Jamison said.

This is not what Ed wanted to hear, and short of producing a gun, which he didn't have, and hijacking the plane, what could he do?

"Well, I understand your position Captain Jamison. You're making a huge mistake, but I accept and respect your decision. I want to tell you that when the plane crashes, everyone will survive the crash if you can get their seatbelts open. I'll help you when the time comes," he said. "At least have everyone tie their seatbelts in a knot, instead of using the buckle; that way you can get everyone out."

"What makes you think there's a problem with the seatbelts?" Jamison asked.

"The newspaper report following the crash said that all the passengers that died did so in their seats with their seatbelts locked," Ed told him.

"Preposterous. There is nothing wrong with the seatbelts. They're brand new and the latest design for quick release. I must ask you, Mr. Drummond, to return to your seat. We'll be landing soon," Jamison said.

Ed stepped past Captain Jamison and returned to his seat next to Nan. Jamison walked past him and returned to the cockpit.

"The captain said no to my request to divert and land the plane. It's going to crash, but you're going to be fine, I'll see to that," Ed told her.

"Ed, how do you know these things? It's as if you truly believe the plane will crash, and now you have me worried that it will," she said.

Captain Jamison came on the PA system and announced that they would be landing very soon and for everyone to please fasten their seatbelts. He also announced the turbulence ahead and that they were just in front of the storm, but not to worry, they would be on the ground long before the rain hits the Stapleton Airfield. Glancing at Nan's wristwatch, Ed saw they had little time. He extended his hands. For some unknown reason she placed her hands in his.

"Nan, you've got to trust me. I want you to live and have a wonderful life. Here is my plan," he said.

Ed told her again that the seatbelt buckles were defective and that hers wouldn't release after the crash. He figured it has something to do with the forces put on the buckle from the crash landing. He told her that she must unbuckle her seatbelt and tie it across her waist instead. Then, as soon as the crash occurred, he would help her untie it and get safely off the burning plane. Glancing at her wristwatch again Ed knew that he had only seven minutes from impact to the final explosion.

"Nan," Ed said, "Please make up your mind. We've only a few minutes to make this right."

Ed could feel the landing gear going down. Nan let go of his hands and unbuckled her seatbelt. She tied it into a knot around her waist with Ed's help. He did the same thing, just to be on the safe side.

It was now close to six pm and the elevator feeling in Ed's stomach was beginning again.

"Here we go. Hang on, Nan," he said as he held her the best he could.

The plane pitched up as before and with engines racing hit the runway. It bounced back into the air and then hit the runway again for good. They were skidding down the runway exactly as they had in Ed's first dream with the grinding sound replacing the engine noise and a trail of sparks following the plane. All this was happening in slow motion for Ed, as his mind was racing. He knew he had enough time to get her out, and maybe, he could help some others out before waking up. He thought to himself, if this works, Nan's obituary wouldn't be in the paper when he looked up the crash tomorrow at the library.

The same bump when the plane hit the fuel truck brought Nan closer to Ed, and then the plane stopped. The screams and yells began again, just at Ed remembered it from the first dream. Nan was dazed but coming back from the shock of the crash. Ed untied his seatbelt and then reached over and untied Nan's.

"Let's get out of here," he said.

Ed stood, grabbed Nan and pulled her to her feet. He held her arms as he walked her backward to the exit door, never taking his eyes off her face for an instant. Stewardess Kimm, standing at the exit door, shouted 'jump and run' as Ed approached. Illuminated by the fire, Ed saw it was only a two-foot jump to the green grass below. He let Nan go, turned and jumped from the plane. He turned to help her climb down, but she wasn't in the doorway. He turned around quickly again to see if she had jumped behind him, but there was only another couple staggering away from the plane.

Ed turned toward the plane again, stepped back and looked over at the window of aisle seat 5A. Someone was in the seat. He saw the orange flames from the fire on the other side of the plane and felt the heat on his face. He quickly stepped over to look in the window and saw Nan. She looked out at him screaming and pointing to her seatbelt. He couldn't hear what she was saying, so he raced back to the exit door.

What went wrong here? She was behind me; why is she back in her seat? He was determined to rescue her, when just as he was stepping back into the plane through the exit door the loud buzzing sound went off in his ears again. He smelled smoke and then heard another high-pitched alarm going off. He put up his hands to cover his ears from the painful noise.

Ed blinked his eyes from the smoke and looked up to see smoke traveling over his head. He jumped up from the futon and, drenched in sweat, raced to the kitchen, opened the oven and pulled out the burning pizza. He tossed it into the sink and turned on the faucet full blast. He then shut off the oven and closed the oven door. He opened the back door to his condo to let the smoke out and after a while the smoke detector finally shut up.

Ed stood in the doorway, taking deep breaths while looking up at the Stapleton control tower with its red blinking light.

"Here it is, the end of my third day in Denver and I almost burn my condo down. What next?" he shouted out loud.

Retreating back into the kitchen, he went to the sink, splashed some water on his face and then turned off the faucet.

"Drummond, what just happened? You had that dream again. You almost saved her!" he said to himself.

Ed glanced at the microwave clock and figured he'd been dreaming for about an hour. His mind raced as he went over every detail of his second dream experience. It was the same basic dream. He changed a few things, including an attempt to save Nan, but the result was the same. He suspected there was more to this than he originally thought. Another force, something unseen, was at play here. He thought he was in control of the dream in his head, but apparently not. He was beginning to think this was someone else's dream; perhaps Nan's and that something else was controlling it. But why was he having it?

Ed had had enough and abruptly stopped thinking about the dream entirely. He cleaned up the mess in the kitchen and went to sleep for the first time in his bedroom, thinking he might have the dream again, but hoping and praying he wouldn't.

Chapter 15

The alarm sounded at six am. It was Tuesday morning and Ed woke after a peaceful night's sleep with no recurrence of the dream. He thought maybe it was finally out of his head, but he still wanted to know what was happening. He felt that Brian could shed light on the subject if persuaded nicely. He also decided to research the crash more thoroughly and thought a repeat trip to the library would fill in the facts and answers he may have overlooked. But first, a morning bike ride would wake him up and clear his mind. Today, his mind needed a lot of clearing.

Dressed in shorts, a rugby shirt and sneakers, Ed patted Big Emma where she was parked broken in the dining room. He made a mental note to find a local bike shop to have her repaired and pulled out his mountain bike for the morning ride. He wanted to explore the neighborhood a little more and to see what was left of the Stapleton Airfield besides the control tower and parking garage.

"That's where I'll start," Ed said to himself. "Let's find the old runways."

He went east on 29th Avenue for a block, then turned north on Unita Street and stopped at MLK Blvd. Across the street on the left was the old Stapleton parking garage and on the right the twelve-story control tower. He rode next to the concrete tower, touched its cool surface and continued east, looking for any trace of the runways. Finding none, because they had all been torn up, he continued until he reached Central Park Blvd. He again turned north and rode slowly, thinking this had to have been were the north-south runway sat. He stopped a quarter-mile up from the control tower, turned around and gazed south, saying to himself, it was right here. His condo complex was off in the distance behind the tower. Ed felt he was very close to a piece of the dream puzzle. Then it hit him.

The DC-3 skidded past the control tower and wound up where his condo was. Perhaps it could be in the exact crash spot.

"That could explain a lot of this," Ed mutters to himself.

This was the first piece of his dream puzzle that made sense. He was sure there was a physical connection between the crash and his condo. Now only the dream itself remained a mystery. He pedaled home as fast as he could, elated to have his first real answer.

He showered, had breakfast, made a few business calls and left for the library at eight-thirty am. He wanted to be there when the doors opened at nine. Arriving at the library, Ed hurriedly walked down the stairs to the basement reference area with his manila folder and again asked the attendant for *The Denver Post* microfiche files from May through December 1952. He started again with the May 24, 1952, issue and read everything again that related to the crash. He printed out the list of survivors and those that perished in the crash. He went to the obituary pages and printed out everything written about those that died.

He did the same for the next day's paper and each issue going forward, printing out articles on anything related to the crash. In the June 1, 1952, issue he stopped and read on the front page a small column caption:

STAPLETON AIRFIELD CRASH

SURVIVOR COMMITS SUICIDE

> Denver – Crash survivor Joan Braly Lorry, 28, was found dead Sunday from a drug overdose. Police spokesman Wendell Smith said her mother, Edith Braly, found Mrs. Lorry's body after failing to meet her to attend church services yesterday at St. Francis Catholic Church. A suicide note revealed she was despondent over the death of her husband, Army Sgt. Steven O. Lorry, who was recently killed in action in Korea. The note stated she wanted to be with him in heaven…

Ed printed out the article and pondered how this woman was miraculously spared in the crash, but chose death as the answer to her situation. He penned a note next to the column that read 'What a tragedy and what irony'.

Ed continued his review of each day's paper, but mention of the crash faded rapidly. Finally, he found and read a July 25, 1952, article on the preliminary crash investigation. The FAA concluded the crash was caused by unexplainable climatic conditions at the time, but the loss of life, except for the co-pilot's death, was due to defective seatbelt buckles manufactured by the Crosley Aircraft Safety Company. Included was a full page of photographs, with several aerial shots taken the day after the crash. Ed could see clearly the runway's end and what appeared to be the 1952 control tower and the field in which the burned plane resided. Further on in the article was a diagram of where the plane rested after the crash. It wasn't to scale, but clearly showed the crash site to be in close proximity to Ed's condo. In his mind this proved the physical connection of the crash to his dream. He printed all the pages.

Next he found a September 30, 1952, column in the business and commerce section that announced the Orland Cattle Company was for sale. It read in part ...President and owner Paul Orland stated it was time to divest the large and growing cattle company. He cited personal reasons for the sale...

Ed printed the article and knew that Nan's death must have devastated the family. One child lost to war, another to a plane crash. These events had clearly taken a toll on the Orland family with what Ed thought was unimaginable grief. A vision of Nan popped into his mind and a thought of visiting her gravesite came into focus. Maybe another piece of the dream puzzle can be found there he thought. Deciding a quick trip to Oaklawn Memorial Park might yield some answers, he gathered all the copies he made and placed them in the manila folder, returned the microfiche box to the attendant and drove to the cemetery after asking her for directions.

Chapter 16

The drive took thirty minutes. The cemetery office staff gave him the directions to Nan's resting place. As he drove slowly along the narrow access road to the oakwood section he questioned himself on why he was somehow compelled to do this, but all logical reason escaped him. He continued on and finally arrived at the approximate grave location and parked. With cemetery map in hand, he walked in the general direction marked with an 'X' on the map. As he walked along he casually read all the names and inscriptions on the grave markers he passed. This was clearly an old section and apparently full for some time. Then he came directly upon Nan's granite headstone. He stopped and felt a slight chill come over him as he read her name with the simple inscription chiseled below in the light colored stone... 'Taken before her time.'

In his mind, Ed had just talked with Nan yesterday. Now the reality of fate and time stared him in the face. Here she was. Ed dwelt again on his last dream noting that he was so close to saving her and if he had succeeded this grave would not be here, or at least not with the date May 23, 1952 chiseled into the stone. Ed bowed his head and whispered to Nan, "I tried to save you twice, but could do nothing to change any of this. I am sorry." Tears formed in his eyes that caught him off guard. How could he mourn a woman he knew only from a dream? Somehow the cemetery visit had ratcheted up his emotional level a notch or two. Soon the tearing stopped and Ed came back to reality more determined than ever to understand what was happening to him and why. The dream had clearly become personal. He walked up to Nan's headstone and touched each letter of her name. Then he backed away from the grave, turned and slowly walked back to his Explorer and drove back to his condo. Along the way he thought that maybe the cemetery visit was not such a good idea. It answered no questions and only succeeded in getting him more deeply involved in the dream.

He did some Chemical Solutions work online after lunch and finally called Teeah at the new office and told her that he would be in for sure tomorrow. As much as he tried to focus on work, his mind continued to take him to the dream and Nan. It was turning into an obsession and interfering in his normal day-to-day life. He found himself Googling dreams and reading everything that came back.

He wanted to further understand what dreams are, where they come from and how they can be interpreted. He typed 'dream intensity' into the search engine to find out how they could become so real, actually spilling over to conscious reality. He got nowhere. So many questions, yet Ed had so few answers. Why had the dream repeated itself? Why could he interact with the dream and talk with Nan, Captain Jamison and Stewardess Kimm? Why was it so real and in such detail? What other forces were at play here and why couldn't he get it out of his mind? Ed wanted it all to end. Finally, he called Brian at the University.

"Hi Brian, it's Ed," he said. "Listen, I'm sorry to bother you at work, but I have more questions to ask you about my dream. It repeated itself again last night and I think I have a piece of the puzzle as to why, but I need you to help me put all this into perspective once and for all."

"You had that crash dream again," Brian said. "You just won't let it go, now will you?"

"I can't seem to get it out of my mind," Ed replied. "The more I try to move on, the more unanswered questions keep popping into my brain about the dream. I'll come over to you house tonight, if it's okay with you."

"Sorry Ed, Sharon is having one of her girlfriends over, but I can stop by after dinner," he said.

"That's great. Say seven pm? And I promise this will be the end of it," Ed replied.

"Sure, sure, sure," Brian laughed back at him. "I'll even bring some books and studies for you to read. Believe it or not, I think I can now put some of this into perspective for you."

"Sounds great", Ed said. "See you at seven."

Ed hit the 'end call' button on his phone and took a big breath and let it out.

"Drummond, you're getting Oscar Charlie," he said out loud, referring to old Vietnam War movie lingo for Out of Control.

Chapter 17

Brian appeared at the door at seven trailing a small rolling suitcase.

Ed opened the door.

"Welcome, amigo. Please enter my dream world," Ed greeted Brian.

Brian laughed, walked in and left the suitcase in the hallway. He followed Ed into the kitchen.

"How about some refreshment?" Ed asked.

"Coors Light," came back from Brian.

Waiting for his beer, he stepped to the rear kitchen window and looked out. He saw the Stapleton control tower and flashing red lights looming overhead.

"So we're standing right on the old airport?" Brian asked.

"Yup," Ed replied, "and I have proof to show you that the 1952 crash site was right here where we're standing."

Ed handed Brian the beer and they both sat down, facing each other across the kitchen table. Ed had his pile of library research all ready to show Brian.

"Okay Ed, let's answer your dream questions," Brian said.

"Brian," Ed began, "I'm grateful you'll listen to me. I'm not crazy and truly want to get this dream behind me once and for all. I think my cycling accident has done something to my brain to make it receptive to this crash incident. I've dreamed the same dream twice, and was able to change my interaction with Nan Orland and the crew in the second dream last night. I tried to change the outcome, but something happened at the last second. I had Nan almost outside the airplane and safe, but something put her back into her seat. Before I could try to save her again I woke up to the smell of burning pizza in the oven with the smoke detector blaring in my ears."

"Ed, you're not crazy and I have news for you; you weren't dreaming a normal dream. I think you were actually there!" Brian told him.

Ed stared back at Brian in disbelief and then asked, "What do you mean I was there?

"Let me explain. During graduate school I took some very fascinating elective courses in parapsychology, which was presented then as the new frontier of psychological research. It was a new way to look at the mind and to offer explanations for paranormal phenomena. I found this subject fascinating at the time, but concluded then and still believe now that there is no scientific way to prove or disprove any of it. And when doubt exists it spawns the most imaginative theories and stories a creative mind could ever want. It stretches the envelope of human possibilities, which is good but in the end it's just mind candy for us young psychologists," Brian said with grin.

"We looked at time travel, all the urban legends, dying in your dreams from the old *Freddy Cougar* movies and more. We even studied remote viewing and other psychological possibilities, such as mental telepathy, clairvoyance, and psychokinesis, like in the Stephen King movie *Carrie.* I call all this pop culture psychology. All this was and still is extremely interesting to me and now it's sort of a hobby. There are psychological phenomena out there that can't be proven or disproven, and God knows, the government tried with their remote viewing experiments in the 1980s to make a breakthrough. Whoever got the money for that research in the name of national security in the Regan era is still a genius, in my mind."

Continuing, Brian said, "In that suitcase I brought all my old books and notes from the classes and case studies we had and my notebook filled with comments, conclusions and my own theories accumulated from over more than ten years. I've got information on psychics, who could give premonitions about the future, and voyeurs, and clairvoyants who could see ghosts and apparitions. And I've analyzed just about every movie based on psychological phenomena made in the last 30 years. What wonderful imaginations those creative authors had to come up with their stories. Tell me; did the movie *Poltergeist* scare the bejesus out of you the first time you saw it?"

Ed nodded yes with a smile.

"All this stuff is interesting, and the pieces of my research that I'm about to share with you may give you answers to your questions, but remember, it is all speculation and can't be proven. However, that notebook is the culmination of my thinking to date, anyway. And I think I've come up with a theory that might explain some or all of what you're experiencing."

Ed sat listening intently to Brian.

"We need some basics to begin. I'm going to briefly go over my concepts of the lifeline and the timeline. Then we'll cover fate and the balance of things and wind up, hopefully, explaining your dream. You stop me at any time, and don't let me bore you. If you're not interested in what I'm saying, I'll stop. Sound like a deal?" Brian said.

"You got it," Ed replied, getting a pen and note pad ready.

"For the human experience on this planet, the lifeline status of being alive or dead are married, or co-exist, at all points through time. It's an either-or status. It moves continuously along the timeline of life, from the beginning of time to eternity. The timeline itself is a moving interface between the past and future that we call the present, or the now. I'm speaking to you in the present right now and we are both alive and moving into the future. This forward movement creates an ever-widening gap between all points in the past and the present. Have I lost you, Ed?" he inquired.

"Not yet," Ed replied.

"Good. Are you familiar with wave theory? I'm sure you studied this in your college physics classes. You remember that sine wave stuff?"

"Of course," Ed said as he took a sip of his Guinness.

"Well, all electronic and sound signals are waves and have a half-life, meaning that their strength diminishes over distance and time. If we stood a quarter-mile apart, you probably couldn't hear a thing I said even if I yelled." Brian continued.

'Ok, nice information, but what's your point?" Ed said getting a little impatient.

"My point, Ed, is that it builds a plausible theory about your dream experience. It is my contention that at the last moment of life, all humans create some sort of psychic energy ball, or signal that contains a message or vision the soon-to-be departed wants to transmit. The conscious or unconscious mind transmits this message at the last moment of life. I think it originates in the exact physical spot someone dies. The strength of the signal is controlled by the circumstances of death and radiates out from there across future living time. For example, an old person dying of natural causes would perhaps leave a behind a very weak signal. Ed, this may not be what you want to hear, but I submit that once dead the dead do nothing. They do not haunt, they do not talk with the living anymore, nothing. I say there is no dead consciousness. Therefore, contrary to common beliefs and superstition, cemeteries contain no psychic energy, as no one died there. They only contain the physical remains. Only in movies and folklore do we see ghosts in graveyards or the dead rising up. This makes for great fiction and great movies, but the dead do nothing. However, I think their psychic signals, created at the point and time of death, move forward in time and can be received by the living.

I'm saying, Ed, that at the moment before death, the individual psychic energy signal for the average human is weak in strength from where it originates from the physical place of death. Let's continue to look at the psychic signal's creation. In my opinion, the signal's strength is proportional to the event, or circumstance, creating it. Thus, the strongest signals would be created in the most traumatic of circumstances where a large number of people died at the same spot and time, such as deaths on the battlefield, death from disasters and death from traumatic situations, such as murder. I think that sometimes individual signals get concentrated or combined to create a single powerful signal or SOS beacon at that point in time. It's something like a gestalt. Mostly, I think these signals remain unconnected and relatively weak," Brian continued.

"Brian, are you trying to tell me that my dream is somehow related to one of these signals my brain has picked up? I got more than a message. So explain to me how I could look right into Nan Orland's eyes, see the strands of her hair and talk with her as if she were right here at this table?" Ed asked in an elevated voice.

Brian responded. "You're getting very close, but no cigar yet. Hang with me a little longer and you'll get your answer. I think the signal is like a VCR recording of a few minutes to perhaps hours of the last moments of life. I don't think it's a 'mind dump' of a person's entire living experience. It tells a very brief story, or leaves a message for the receiver to understand. The signal is created by the human mind and transmitted at that point in time to the future and can only be received, stored, decoded and played back by the human mind.

Ed, I think you received a concentrated SOS signal from those that died on the plane. I estimate that these concentrated human psychic signals are very rare, with a one in a million chance of happening, and these signals, or messages across time, captured in the last moments of life are what people in the future may receive. When their minds decode the signal they can have dreams or visions. I think this explains what a lot of clairvoyants say they experience when they say they see a ghost, or feel the presence of a ghost. They just receive the signal and it plays back in their mind." Brian exclaimed.

"I think transmitting the concentrated signal is easy compared to the ability to receive the message. I would say that ninety-nine percent plus of all the signals go un-received and over time grow weaker and weaker. The human ability to receive these signals, decode and play them back is also very rare, and again, I think in the million to one range. I also believe the transmitted signal can be received by an electronic device like a TV or radio, perhaps as white noise combined with every other signal out there, across all the frequencies possible, but it takes the human mind to receive, decode, or decipher the encrypted message. Otherwise, it just remains static and noise," Brian said and paused.

Ed was furiously taking notes and trying to grasp these concepts and ideas as fast as Brian was rolling them off his tongue, but it was taxing his mental abilities and he was on the verge of information overload.

"Ed, somewhere in our brain, in all our brains, is a secret room that we can't get to consciously, that controls our ability to receive these psychic signals; it's the same place from which our final message is transmitted. Having the ability to receive and decipher these messages across time is a rare gift that only a few in the living world possess. It's a blessing and curse at the same time. Imagine having this ability turned on all the time – and my friend, I think yours has been turned on. For example, if you pass a fatal auto accident site, you get a message popping into your brain. The closer you are on the timeline to the event the stronger the signal. I am not sure if the conscious mind can decipher these signal messages, but the unconscious mind surely can. If this were my fate, I would be wearing aluminum foil on my head all the time to keep this stuff out of my brain! You do have a roll of foil here in the kitchen for emergency use?" Brian quipped.

Both Ed and Brian had a good laugh and enjoyed a sip of their brews.

"Remember Ed, these are just messages or recordings and not the real thing. The strongest signal is in the exact physical spot of the death event," he said.

"Are you finally suggesting," Ed began, "that I have been dreaming a recording of that 1952 airplane crash transmitted from the past?"

Brian smiled and said, "Not exactly, my friend. As I said before, I think you were actually there."

Ed looked straight at Brian, utterly confused and not grasping what he was saying.

"Please back up and explain your last statement to me very slowly," Ed said.

"Okay, read my lips. I think your head injury unlocked your secret room's ability to receive these signals across time. However, the concentrated SOS signal from your 1952 airplane crash did something extra special. Not only did you receive it, but it drew your mind back in time to the source," Brian asserted.

"You said before it was a recording. How does that relate to being there? Ed asked.

"As I said, the closer your mind got to the signal's source, the stronger the signal. Now you say the plane ended up right here where your condo is fifty-five years ago. So we've eliminated distance from the equation and are only talking about time. When your mind reached the timeline of May 23,1952, at this very spot, it popped over to the living side of the living-or-dead equation. This means that Ed, you were actually experiencing that last hour of living reality with all those souls on the plane. How fantastic is that! Ed, you've gone back and touched that reality even if only for a short time. What a mind trip you had! The essence of your very being was there. And yes, I believe that you were actually talking with Nan Orland and she with you," Brian exclaimed, smiling profusely.

Ed sat back in his chair for a moment, trying to fully absorb all these concepts and ideas, as well as Brian's final revelation that Ed had really been there and that somehow he had traveled back to 1952. He wondered why he didn't feel fantastic and elated about this special gift. It left him with an empty, searching feeling inside that he couldn't quite understand.

"I don't feel fantastic about this, but at least you don't think I'm crazy after all," Ed said.

"No Ed, you're not crazy. I do want to get down several pages about you in my notebook, if not a whole notebook to yourself, but you are not crazy. You've somehow created a time portal to the past and this gift is exciting and needs exploring. Are you game to be my guinea pig on this, Ed?" Brian exclaimed.

Both men laughed again, hoisted their glasses and sipped their brews.

"Now, I have more theory for you, Ed, to explain why you couldn't change anything in the past. The word is fate and the orderly balance of things. You weren't supposed to be there, but somehow you got there. Fate is very finicky, whoever he or she is. Fate may even be God for all we know, with the job of keeping everything in the past nice and tidy. And remember this Ed – you can't cheat fate," Brian said.

"Okay, so I was there and you say fate put Nan back into her seat in my second dream? Ed said.

"You got it. Nothing can change the past. You wanted to save your new friend Nan, but that would put one more life over on the living side of the crash. It's impossible to do. Now how many people were on the plane?" Brian asked.

"There were twenty souls on the plane. Seven were saved and thirteen died." Ed held up his copy of the front page of *The Denver Post.*

"See Ed, you tried to mess with the living-and-dead equation and fate intervened. Pushing your new girlfriend over to the living side couldn't be allowed. It would be out of balance in the grand scheme of things."

"So how do I fix this the next time I have the dream?" Ed blurted out.

"That's the sixty-four thousand dollar question I hope you leave alone. You can't change anything in the past. If the dream comes back again I hope you just enjoy it as your personal holodeck, like in Star Trek. You'll always wake up here in your condo safe and sound after the most fantastic dating experience any bachelor could ever want. Why not just let it go at that Ed? Just leave it alone is my advice," Brian said.

"Brian, you're probably right. Leaving all this alone is best. I now think I fully understand what happened to me and appreciate your patience in giving me the most logical explanation possible. I guess I'll just leave it alone, as you say. And you know, I think I found the exact point or epicenter of the signal, which is directly where my futon is in the living room. Both my dreams happened while I was dozing or asleep on the futon. Last night I slept like a baby in my bedroom dream-free," he said.

"See what I mean Ed? We put a logical explanation together for your dream and all your questions about it are now answered. Say, I gotta go. Sharon will kill me if I stay out too late. I've a full day tomorrow and need to get some shut eye myself. I know you may still want to look over the stuff in my suitcase on all this so I'll leave it with you. Promise me Ed, your dreaming days are coming to an end? Right, Ed?"

"Yes Brian, I promise to be a good boy and let the dream go," Ed said. "With your most excellent analysis it's practically out of my mind as we speak."

Both men had another good laugh. Brian stood, shook Ed's hand and walked toward the front door, glancing at the futon in the living room on his way out. He said goodbye. Ed closed the front door, grabbed the handle on the suitcase and returned to the kitchen table and his notes. Thoughts of a final Nan Orland rescue mission were beginning to form in Ed's mind as he sat back down.

Chapter 18

Ed reviewed his hastily written notes and circles the word gift several times. Brian's earlier dream revelations had had a profound effect on him and for the first time he questioned what to do with his new gift. Should I just drop all this as Brian has suggested and resume my new life in Denver, or should I pursue the dream further? He pondered the idea of having unlocked a secret room in his brain that begged to be explored. Ed likened this to finding an open bank vault; he had to decide whether to close the door and spin the tumbler, or explore what was inside. He made his decision. The gift would be used in one final attempt to rescue Nan Orland across time or simply to say goodbye. Either way, it would be the end of this and for all he knew the dream might never occur again once his brain healed from the crash.

"At least I can try to save her one more time," Ed said out loud, without yet knowing how it could be done.

He put a quick list together of the challenges he faced in accomplishing his final rescue mission and began to address each one thoroughly and methodically. Last shots are last shots and must be planned meticulously he thought to himself.

First on the list was how to deal with fate and messing with the living or dead equation. Brian told him nothing in the past could be changed, as that messes with life's balance. Ed reasoned that if the equation had to be in balance, then one of the survivors could be substituted for Nan. Someone must not get off, or someone must be put back on board in Nan's place. He found and studied the list of seven saved persons: Mr. and Mrs. Gibson, Jack Moser, Mr. and Mrs. Conway, Dodie Cullen and Joan Lorry. He circled Joan Lorry's name. He remembered her shouting to Captain Jamison that she wanted to die and join her husband in heaven while he carried her out of the plane to safety. Ed looked in his folder and found the headline of her tragic suicide a week after being saved, and concluded that her being saved in the crash only postponed her desire to be with her husband in heaven. Moving up her death was the logical thing to do. Ed started to think how Joan Lorry could be kept in her seat and not rescued by Jamison. He would have to intervene somehow and prevent her from leaving the aircraft.

"What am I saying," Ed blurted out. "I can't play God like this."

Realizing what he was suggesting in such a logical, expedient and clinical fashion caught him off guard. It soon became a repugnant idea and he quickly tried to stop that train of thought. While substituting Joan Lorry for Nan Orland was a logical choice, he had no grounds to do so. Then it hit him. The newspaper clipping said Joan was Catholic. That meant her subsequent suicide prevented her from going to heaven to be with her husband. Keeping her on the plane to die would allow her to be with her husband at the end of the day. He was actually doing her a favor. Now he had at least some flimsy moral justification to keep Joan on the plane in substitution for Nan, but he still needed to focus how to do this. He could interfere with Captain Jamison and foil Joan's rescue. That would work. Ed tossed his pencil down and stood up. He walked outside to his back porch and stared up at the Stapleton control tower in frustration.

"Damn dream," Ed shouted out to the darkness as loud as he could.

He took a deep breath and let it all out. His mind was racing. He had grown such strong feelings for Nan that his compelling desire to save the one he loved was clouding his judgment and his very being. He would do anything to save her, but not at the expense of another person. Drawing a line in your dreams was new thinking for Ed. Even with logical and moral justification he decided to leave Joan alone. Maybe all this was a test of his character, or a quest for some unknown truth for which he had been unconsciously searching. In any event, this substitution scheme of one person for another was out.

"Okay Drummond," he muttered out loud, "you've been up against the wall before and have always pulled it off. This is going to be your finest solution ever. Just change the score."

Dismissing a hijack attempt as nuts, Ed decided to leave most everything in his second dream as before, but personally push Nan off the plane to safety and immediately return to her seat to prevent fate from putting her back. Two people can't occupy the same space, so he would be the seat linebacker until he woke up. So the score will change to eight and twelve when I go to the library again. I think 1952 can absorb one more living person. He remembered Brian's warning that you can't cheat fate, but he reasoned that his very presence in 1952 was proof that anything was possible in a dream.

"After all, three times is the charm."

With that new scenario Ed became charged again and returned to the kitchen table and to his notes with the hope that his foolproof rescue plan would work. Next on his list was dream duration time and waking up on the futon. Thinking this through, he only remembered waking up in the morning after his first dream, so he had no idea when the dream really began. In the second dream he remembered lying on the futon with the pizza timer and smoke alarm waking him up after fifty-five minutes of sleep. He also remembered Captain Jamison saying the plane would land in less than an hour, so obviously the dream's 'play time' was just about one hour; therefore, he had to have some sort of mechanical means to wake up in 2007 after he saved Nan in 1952. Something mechanical and fail-safe, he repeated to himself. His primary wake up device would be the travel alarm clock, and for a failsafe he thought about something to tip the futon so he'd roll off onto the floor. Quickly, he decided to use his electric bicycle air compressor fitted to the pneumatic bottle jack he had in the garage. He would just put another light timer on the compressor to come on in one hour; that would raise the jack piston and tip the futon, rolling him off to a startling wake up on the floor if the alarm failed.

Ed jumped up. Within minutes he returned to the living room from the garage with his air compressor, the bottle jack, an electric cord, the timer and some duct tape. He assembled his simple contraption and placed the bottle jack piston under the back beam of the futon. He then taped it to hold it in place. For a test he set the timer for about one minute, plugged the compressor into the timer, the timer into the cord and the cord into the wall outlet. Then he went to the front of the futon and taped both legs to the floor to be sure they wouldn't slide.

He laid down on the futon to test his contraption and closed his eyes. Sure enough, the timer clicked and the compressor came on and he felt the back of the futon rising until he rolled off onto the floor.

"Terrific," Ed said out loud as he got up and turned off the compressor. He lowered the bottle jack piston. "We're done."

Since it was now close to midnight, he called it a night and retired to his bedroom; it was the end of day four in Denver and he was close to the edge.

Chapter 19

Ed woke Wednesday morning in his bedroom at six to the travel alarm giving off its normal buzzing sound. Shutting it off, he looked out the window and saw that is was going to be another beautiful, sunny day in Denver.

He pulled on his cycling workout outfit, shoes and helmet, and headed to the dining room where Big Emma leaned broken and unhappy against the wall. He patted her seat, grabbed his trail bike and headed out the front door for a thirty-minute ride to wake up, clear his thoughts and get focused for the day. Going east on 29th Place he looked left to view the Stapleton control tower standing tall in the morning sun. He continued to ride hard for fifteen minutes down Route 83 and then turned around and headed back home.

After showering and finishing breakfast Ed fired up his laptop on the kitchen table and began to answer e-mails. He made a list of phone calls he had to make and added Brian

Edmonds' name to the end. His cell phone chirped and he saw that was his boss, Pat Hamilton, who probably wanted a progress update on setting up the office. Sure enough, the questions were rapid fire: Did you hire the office person, Teeah? Did you get the furniture I ordered yet? Are the phones installed and what about the business license application? Payroll wants the employment application and forms for Teeah faxed in today. Ed responded to each question and finally found a moment to tell Pat about his bicycle accident the previous Sunday and how the doctor told him to take it easy for two days, which he had done and was now good as new and charging ahead with getting the office set up. They talked about the Scholle Chemical Co. disposal project and Ed promised to contact them and set up an appointment to visit to get the project going. The focus on work was refreshing and made him feel comfortable and in his zone again. Hamilton gave him the rest of the week to sort out all the office admin details and Ed promised he would get it done. "Not to worry, boss," was the last thing he said before ending the call.

In less than an hour Ed had responded to his e-mails and made all his calls, except one. He stopped and circled Brian's name. He wanted to call to tell him that he was going to try hooking up with the dream again that evening, but he hesitated in dialing and closed his cell phone without making the call.

He got out the Scholle Chemical file from his black canvas briefcase and worked on that project until lunchtime. His confidence and general positive attitude had been building all morning. The total focus on work somehow gave him renewed strength. Maybe getting caught up and back on top of his game was what he needed. Positive favorable outcomes were what he liked to achieve, in his business affairs anyway.

After lunch he drove to the office to see Teeah and check on how she was getting along organizing the office. He also would check on that payroll paperwork and fax it to Chicago, and he also wanted to try to give her an orientation to the company and her job. Teeah was twenty-three and a single mother. To Ed's surprise, when he got there her two-year-old son was in the office, sitting on the floor next to her reception desk. Kids in the Chicago office were taboo and he wasn't sure at first how to handle the situation. She told him the little fellow was sick and that she couldn't take him to day care; she couldn't stay home, because she needed the money, and since Ed also needed her to get the office up and running, she had made the decision to bring him in. Ed told her he appreciated her dedication and desire to get the job done, but that she needed to be home with her son. Ed sent her home after promising to pay her for the day and to call him in the morning if she needed to stay home tomorrow. Teeah thanked him for understanding, said goodbye, and gathered up her son and left.

Ed went into his new office, clicked on the lights and tried out his new chair. The smell of new leather permeated the room. He sat down, kicked back and put his feet up on the new cherry desk, smiled and thought of how wonderful it is when a plan comes together.

Noticing the new telephone on his desk, he lifted the receiver and hit an outside line.

"Let's give Brian a call and give him an update," Ed said as he fumbled to get the number from his cell phone.

Ed got Brian's voicemail and left him a short message. Hanging up, Ed left his office and began to survey the entire office space. He made a list of things for Teeah to do the next morning and left it on her desk. At half past four he locked up the office and drove back to his condo.

En route, his cell phone began to chirp. He saw that it was Brian calling and opened the phone.

"Hello my friend. Thanks for returning my call. Do you have a minute?" Ed cordially inquired with a grin.

"You sound great today Ed, not your normal dream, panicky self. What's got you in such a good mood?" Brian asked.

"Well, for starters I've been focusing on my new life here in Denver and my job, and that seems to have gotten me in a good mood. However, after thinking everything over we covered last night I did want to share with you some thoughts on my dream. And don't get mad, I just want you to hear about my new plan," Ed said.

"What plan are you conjuring up Ed?" Brian responded.

The roles were subtly reversed; Ed was in good spirits and Brian slightly on edge.

"I'm going to try the dream experience one more time to say goodbye to Nan," Ed told him, omitting the new rescue scheme details.

"Aren't you pushing this a little too hard? Remember, you promised me last night you would let this all go. Ed, you were awakened out of your dream the last two times pretty dramatically. What will wake you out of this one? You sure don't want to be a crispy critter in 1952 and dead on a futon in 2007, do you? I want you to cease and desist on the dream or there could be dire circumstances. Can't you just enjoy and reflect on the two dream experiences you had in meeting Nan and getting to know her? One more trip back there is not going to change anything. And besides, what makes you think your brain will 'connect' with the SOS signal, first thing? As your new parapsychologist I am prescribing a night out on the town with some real live people to bring you back to earth."

Ed cracked up and laughed, but sensed Brian's seriousness to leave well enough alone.

"Not to worry. I've got everything under control with a failsafe wakeup system to bring me back okay. I think I can control everything, even connecting to the signal, as you say. Look, my brain may be fully healed by tomorrow and the gift could be gone; this is one way to find out. It would be my luck that the dream won't happen again, but don't deny me one more attempt to see Nan. I have to do this to get her out of my mind. Listen, why don't you come over tomorrow night and baby sit? The trip only takes an hour or so," he told Brian, not letting him know that the plan was for Ed to go alone that evening.

"Sure. Great idea, Ed. I can observe and monitor what you're doing, which should add peace of mind for both of us. What time do you intend to set sail?" Brian asked.

"The dream leaves port at seven-thirty pm sharp, tomorrow. I intend to be up early and have an exhausting day to make me really physically tired. A glass of Guinness administered thirty minutes prior to sailing will put me soundly to sleep at the appointed hour," Ed jokingly tossed back to Brian.

"At least you'll have adult supervision," Brian retorted.

"See you tomorrow. Take care," Ed said and closed his cell phone. He didn't want to lie to Brian, but going this alone was the better solution, from his perspective.

Ed arrived home around five-thirty pm, parked his Explorer in the garage and walked into the condo. He immediately stopped and looked at the futon, which had now taken on the aura of a space capsule. He almost felt that he should be putting on a space suit for his next mission to the past, but the Chicago Bears sweats would do just fine. He smiled at the air compressor and jack contraption and knew that he could make it all happen, if the gift was still with him.

He went into the kitchen, turned on the light and saw the suitcase and his notebook and manila folder stuffed with the newspaper copies sitting on the kitchen table. He removed a can of Guinness from the fridge, opened it, and poured it into a large mug. He sat down, took a big swallow and set it down. He reached for a felt tipped pen and wrote something on the front of the manila folder in big script and then took it to the living room and placed it on the coffee table. Ed went to his bedroom, pulled on his Bears sweats and remembered to splash some Bay Rum on his face. Nan's favorite! He grabbed the travel alarm clock and returned to the living room and set it on the coffee table. He went into the kitchen to finish his mug of Guinness and returned to the living room.

He set his digital travel alarm clock to go off in one hour and thirty minutes and the compressor timer to come on after the same amount of time; the extra half hour was for Ed to relax and doze off. With his failsafe wakeup devices ready he lay down on the futon, propped his head up with a pillow and folded his arms across his chest. He took a deep breath, exhaled and closed his eyes. The Guinness was doing its job, giving him a way to immediately relax and get ready to receive the signal. He thought of Nan, and how much he loved her; he realized there was probably nothing he could do to save her, but he would give it a try. Little did Ed know that his brain's secret room receivers were already receiving the SOS signal and that he would 'connect' the moment he drifted off to sleep.

Ed continued to think about his plan to save Nan. Somehow Brian's words of dire consequences popped into his thoughts, making him wonder if all this was a bad idea. Damn it, Ed thought, it's back and forth, left brain, right brain, turn to the left, turn to the right, standup, sit down fight, fight, fight. He opened his eyes and saw his living room ceiling. Maybe the gift was gone. Glancing over to the travel clock he saw that twenty-five minutes had elapsed since he lay down. He closed his eyes again and began a countdown: ten nine eight seven six five four three two one blastoff. Ed felt the futon moving slightly and thought there must be something wrong with the air compressor timer coming on too soon. He opened his eyes to investigate and found himself seated in very familiar surroundings.

Chapter 20

The third time's a charm; Ed wanted to savor every moment of his dream experience as it brought him across to the living side of the lifeline and timeline on May 23, 1952. The drone of the DC-3 engines was music to his ears. The lavatory was still small and impossible for him to fully stand up in, so he remained hunched over and looked into the mirror wearing a big grin. He felt like a kid locked in a bicycle store. This time, for fun, he turned on the water in the sink, unwrapped a bar of soap and washed his hands. Then he took one of the United Airlines towels and dried them, and when finished he put the towel into the basket.

"Okay Drummond, its show time," he said quietly to himself as he reached for the door lever and slowly pushed it down. He stepped out and closed the door behind him.

Ed wanted to cut to the chase in this third dream but knew he had to go through the motions again. After all, it was the third time repeating everything for him, but still the first time for everyone else on the plane. He was beginning to feel like Bill Murray in the movie *Groundhog Day*; the thought brought another smile to his face. He had to get it right the third time, too. Just as before, Stewardess Kimm noticed him standing by the lavatory and moved down the aisle right up to him, starting the cycle again.

"Where did you come from?" she asked, with the same inquisitive look.

"In there," Ed replied pointing back to the lavatory. "In there."

"Listen mister, did you get on in Omaha?" she asked.

"No, Miss Kimm, I just came from the year 2007," he said.

"You must be a stowaway then," she said. "And what is your name, sir?"

"I'm Ed Drummond and I live in Denver and want to talk with Captain Jamison immediately. I've something very important to tell him. It's a matter of life or death."

Stewardess Kimm looked at him in the same curious fashion, trying to figure out how he could know her name and that of Captain Jamison.

"Please come with me," she said.

Ed followed her up the aisle, but he slowed to look at everyone on the plane and to make note of where the vacant seats were. He knew their names, but didn't know how to match them up, except for Nan and Joan Lorry. The stewardess stopped at aisle five and turned around.

"Please sit down here while I notify the captain," she said.

Ed nodded, glanced over at Joan Lorry across the aisle and sat down next to Nan. Just as before, Nan was looking out the window when Ed sat down and her head was turning to see who was next to her. Ed had memorized everything about this wonderful first experience and hoped it would play out the same. Her head turned towards him and their eyes met again, just like before. She stared at him; he stared at her, saying nothing. Soon Nan extended her hand and introduced herself.

"Hello, I'm Nan Orland. I don't think I noticed you before," she said.

He extended his hand and he held hers ever so lightly.

"I'm Ed Drummond from Denver, Colorado," he said.

"Well that makes two of us, Mr. Drummond," she replied, smiling brightly. Ed smiled back.

One thing was constant in all these dream experiences; he could not stop looking at her lovely face. Ed wanted to remember every facet of it, her hair, her entire being. Remembering how embarrassed he was in the second dream by not letting go of her hand, he appropriately let go at the right instant this time.

"May I call you Nan?" he asked.

"Of course you can," Nan replied.

"Nan, I'm from the future," he said, but before he could finish his sentence again Captain Jamison was tapping him on the shoulder. Stewardess Kimm stood beside him.

"I'm Captain Jamison. Would you please step to the rear of the plane for a moment?"

Ed got up from his seat and walked down the aisle to the back of the plane. Jamison looked at him for a moment without speaking.

"Mr. Drummond, Stewardess Kimm informs me you are a stowaway. Is that so?" he said.

"No sir, I'm not. This may be hard for you to believe, but I'm from the year 2007 and have been sent back here to warn you that this plane will crash on landing in Denver during a severe thunderstorm that will push the plane down on the runway hard. You can't recover from the severe downdraft. Ten passengers, you and Miss Kimm here will die if you don't divert now to another airport," Ed repeated his speech from memory as best he could.

Captain Jamison gave Stewardess Kimm a look, confirming that they had a mental case on board.

"Mr. Drummond, I no doubt believe you want to save my plane and passengers from harm. I will call Denver control and verify the severe weather conditions you predict and will take your diversion request under advisement with United's Operation Center in Chicago. Is that fair?" Jamison said.

"Yes Captain Jamison, please proceed," Ed replied, expressionless. Jamison asked Ed to return to his seat and assured Ed that he would radio for instructions. Captain Jamison walked back up the aisle to the cockpit. Ed followed, glancing over to look at Joan Lorry in seat 5C before sitting down next to Nan.

"Mind explaining what all that was about, Mr. Drummond?" she asked.

Ed started from the beginning and went through the entire story of being from the year 2007. Nan responded with the same questions and doubting laughs as before. He repeated everything about his move to Denver, the bicycle accident, how they've met twice before in his dream, which is not really a dream, but something that gets him back to her in 1952. He talked about her family, her job and trip to Chicago, but he stopped short again before revealing the plane crash and her death.

"May I call you Ed?" she asked.

"Of course," he replied.

"Ed, you seem well informed about me, but nothing that hasn't been in the newspapers before. These other matters you talk about I don't think I fully understand," she said.

Ed replied, "Well, I know your prize bull named Topper just won best of show in Chicago."

Ed felt her look at his eyes and face as never before. This was the moment, the exact moment things clicked for Nan and she knew he was the one for her. Whatever it was – it just happened. She now understood completely Joan Lorry's comment about how 'just one look into each others eyes' was all it would take to know you were truly meant for each other. Then Ed said the same thing that would change everything.

"Nan, I'm here on a rescue mission to save you if I can."

"What do you mean save me? Save me from what?" she asked.

He explained again the upcoming crash, the defective seatbelt that would hold her trapped in her seat, unless tied. He explained that seven people were saved, including Joan Lorry across the aisle, and that thirteen would die, including her. He went over the timeline and lifeline concepts and how he tried to save her last time, but that fate put her back into her seat. This time he would occupy her seat in the plane so fate could not put her back. He explained to her how he wanted to save everyone on the plane, but that it was impossible and to just trust him that he was telling the truth. Nan listened to him intently and remained expressionless until Ed had finished. Then the smile came back to her face.

"You paint a very interesting picture, Ed," she said, still listening intently. "How did you escape before from this dream?"

"As the plane exploded I woke up on my couch in 2007, both times," he replied.

Just then Captain Jamison came down the aisle, looked at Ed and pointed to the back of the plane. Ed turned to Nan.

"Hold on. There's more and I'll be right back," he said as he stood up and walked to the back of the plane.

Turning around near the exit door they looked at each other before Captain Jamison speaks.

"I have called Denver control. They confirm a thunderstorm is approaching, but it's not expected until after we land. It's dry as a bone at the field now. Chicago confirms the weather forecast and will not authorize a diversion. This plane will land safely in Denver, and on time Mr. Drummond. We'll go over your prophecy and flight theories on the ground. I'm sorry, but I must follow my orders."

"Well, I understand your position, Captain Jamison. You're making a huge mistake, but I accept and respect your decision," Ed said, omitting his prior reference to the defective seatbelts.

"I must ask you, Mr. Drummond, to return to your seat. We'll be landing soon," Jamison said.

Ed stepped past Captain Jamison and returned up the aisle to his seat. Jamison walked past him and returned to the cockpit. Ed turned to Nan.

"The captain said no to my request to divert the flight and land at another airport. It's going to crash from the storm, but you're going to be fine, I'll see to that," Ed said.

"How do you know these things?" Nan questioned. "It's as if you truly believe the plane will crash, and now you have me worried that it will."

"Nan, you've got to trust me. I love you and want you to live a wonderful long life. It's my gift to you, if we can pull it off and get you off this plane. We're never going to have any more time together than what we have right now," Ed said.

Nan was practically breathless from trying to absorb everything Ed was saying. She looked at him dumbfounded, not knowing how to respond.

"Listen Nan, I've got to get something just in case," he exclaimed, remembering that a dinner knife or spoon might come in handy for prying the seatbelt mechanism.

Ed stepped abruptly into the aisle at the exact time Stewardess Kimm was coming up the aisle with a tray of cups, glasses and ashtrays. They collided and everything on the tray came crashing down on the back of Joan Lorry's seat, soaking her dress with the liquids and covering her with cigarette ashes. Joan immediately stood up and stared at Stewardess Kimm, who apologized profusely. She asked Joan to move up to seat 4C while she ran up the aisle to the galley to get a towel. Ed sat back down and looked at vacant seat 5C, covered in the tray, cups, glasses and cigarette butts. He watched as Joan Lorry moved forward to seat 4C and sat down. Stewardess Kimm raced back down the aisle with several towels and began to blot the back of Joan's black dress. Apologies continued to pour from her mouth.

Ed was trying to understand what had just happened when Captain Jamison came on the PA system to announce that they would be landing very soon and for everyone to please fasten their seatbelts. He also announced the turbulence ahead and that they were just in front of the storm, but not to worry, they would be on the ground long before the rains hit Stapleton Airfield.

Just then the plane shuddered as it entered the outer air bands of the storm. Glancing at Nan's wristwatch, he saw it was again close to six pm. He turned in his seat to face Nan and extended his hand. She instinctively placed her hand in his.

"Nan," Ed said, "please make up your mind. We've only a few minutes to make this right. Three times is a charm."

Ed could feel the landing gear going down again. Nan let go of his hands and unbuckled her seatbelt. She tied it into a knot with Ed's help. Ed did the same thing, as before. It was now six pm and the elevator feeling in Ed's stomach was beginning.

"Here we go. Hang on Nan," he said, as he held her the best he could.

The plane pitched up as before and with engines racing hit the runway, bounced back into the air and then smacked the runway again for good. They were sliding down the runway exactly as in both previous dreams with the grinding sound replacing the engine noise and a trail of sparks following the plane as it skidded down the runway. The same bump brought Nan closer to Ed as the plane sliced into the fuel truck; then the plane stopped. The screams and yells began again. Ed looked over at Nan who was dazed, but coming back from the shock of the crash. Ed untied his seatbelt and then reached over and untied Nan's.

"Let's get you out of here," Ed told Nan as he stood. He pulled her to her feet and walked her backward to the exit door, never taking his eyes off her face for an instant.

At the doorway, he unexpectedly kissed her and handed her off to Stewardess Kimm, who helped Nan off the plane, shouting 'jump and run.' Ed watched her run across the grass and told Stewardess Kimm he would help to free the other passengers. Instead, he returned to Nan's seat, sat down and buckled himself in. This would be a good time to wake up, he thought, as the explosion was just around the corner. He had forgotten all about Joan Lorry in the crash confusion and when he looked over he noticed that she appeared unconscious in her new seat. He unbuckled his seatbelt, jumped up and moved over to her seat to try and free her, just as Captain Jameson came up the aisle and stopped next to him.

"Let me in there," Jamison barked, pushing Ed aside.

Jamison saw that she was unconscious and reached down to unlock her seatbelt buckle, but it was frozen like the others. Ed stood watching as Jamison struggled to free Joan Lorry. This wasn't to happen this way. Joan was to be saved. Mindful that fate could switch things back as it had before, Ed moved past Captain Jamison and got back into Nan's seat. Before he could buckle up, Jamison was standing over him.

"How did you know this was going to happen?" he shouted at Ed. "Everything you said to me before came true." At the same time he reached over and grabbed Ed's right arm.

"Come on, you're getting out of here now," Jamison shouted as Ed struggled to remain where he was.

"No, no leave me here and get the others out first," he yelled back.

Ed continued to think of the balance equation and didn't want anything to mess it up at this point, particularly by his exiting the burning plane. After all, he was due to wake up and be on his futon in a minute and all this would be over forever, or so he thought. While Ed figured fate's living or dead equation was in balance with Joan trapped in her seat and Nan safe outside, it was not supposed to happen this way. Jamison, more determined than ever, tried to drag Ed out of his seat.

They struggled and Ed tried to remove Captain Jamison's grip from his arms. Finally, he pried Jamison's hand from his right arm, but what came next was unexpected. The punch hit Ed hard in the right temple and he immediately crumpled in his seat. Captain Jamison placed both arms around him and pulled him backwards down the aisle to the exit door. Ed was dazed and for those few moments and could do nothing to stop the strong arms dragging him to the door. Ed found himself flying through the air after having been thrown out the DC-3's exit door by the combined effort of Jamison and Kimm. All this happened in slow motion. Ed could see green ahead, lots of green grass, and he found himself crash landing on the soft wet grass and tumbling over to land flat on his back. His eyes were wide open. He lay motionless and seemed paralyzed, but he could see the night sky, hear the sirens, smell the smoke and see the flicker of the flames around him. Now would be the time to wake up. Where is the buzzing alarm? The futon should tip any time soon and this will be over.

Chapter 21

"Wake up Drummond, wake up!" he mumbled out loud while lying on the wet grass, but nothing happened.

Someone approached and stared down at him.

"Ed, is that you?" Nan asked.

Ed was speechless, but immediately recognized Nan's voice and face in the flicking light.

"Yes, it's me."

She reached for his arms, and began to drag him backwards, away from the burning plane. This was very confusing to Ed; it wasn't the way he planned it. He was to wake up while on the plane and return to 2007, none the worse for wear, but something had changed in the equation. He continued to look at Nan's face.

"Nan, I can get up. Please help me up," he said.

She let go of his arms and helped Ed to his feet. She placed one of his arms over her shoulder and they began to swiftly walk away from the plane. Just then, the Super DC-3 behind them exploded in a fireball of flames. The explosion knocked Nan and Ed to the ground, where they landed face down and intertwined. They were both breathing heavily from the exertion of the fast walk and lay still for a moment on the wet grass looking at each other silently in the bright flickering light, arms still holding each other. Ed moved closer to Nan and kissed her. They embraced a moment more and slowly separated. Both remained silent, looking at each other for a minute that seemed to go on forever. Ed touched her hair. She touched the side of his face. Then Ed smiled at Nan, and she smiled back.

"Let's get out of here," he said as he stood up and pulled Nan to her feet.

They held hands and slowly walked away from the burning plane, oblivious to all the rescue activity going on around them. It was as if they both existed in a bubble, safe and separate from the world around them. They walked towards the distant airport terminal building in silence.

Ed knew he loved Nan, but this was not supposed to be happening. He would surely wake up at any moment and be on the floor in his apartment fifty-five years in the future. They continued to walk to the front of the airport terminal, where Ed spotted a lone cab, the driver nowhere to be found. He peered through the driver's window, spied the keys in the ignition and motioned for Nan to jump in the front seat.

"Not so fast, Mr. Drummond. I'll drive," Nan said.

So Ed went around the car to the passenger side, while Nan got in and started up the motor.

"I'm taking you home," he heard Nan say as he climbed into the passenger seat.

Pulling away from the curb Ed looked at the three speed column shifter that Nan was moving through the gears.

"Good decision, I've never driven a stick shift like that before," he said.

She smiled and chuckled but kept her eyes on the road. "Don't you future people drive cars anymore?" she asked.

Ed reached over and touched Nan's right hand on the steering wheel. She glanced over at him. Ed continued to wonder what had happened, how it was possible that he was in 1952. Is this a dream too? But how could it be? The dream experience was only an hour long and surely more time than that had gone by. Ed was flooded with questions again. Could this be another reality?

Nan drove the cab along the two-lane highway toward downtown Denver. Ed reached over several more times and touched her hand and then her cheek. She seemed real to him and her skin was soft and warm to the touch.

"Ed, I don't know what just happened back there, but everything you said on the plane about the crash came true. If I really died before you came along, I seem to be alive now – and so are you. I guess I should thank you for saving my life, or something," she said.

Ed's mind raced at full throttle. What had just happened, what was happening, and why was he still here in 1952 with Nan? Was it just another dream he would wake up from, or was this somehow different? Ed looked at the streetlights along the two-lane highway they were traveling on when the answers all came to him. The minute Captain Jamison hit him in the head it must have broken the connection to the future. At that instant his entire being shifted to 1952 on the living side of the equation, to where his mind was. Not even fate could change this back; however, Joan Lorry's fate changed and kept the crash living or dead equation in balance. Ed realized his indirect responsibility for causing her to move up a seat, but he knew he had never intended to do her harm and knew now she was finally in heaven with her husband.

"Nan," he said, "somehow I managed to change both our fates today. I've been searching for you all my life, and I found you in a dream. Now, we're together. I'm not sure where we go from here, or if this is just a dream I'll wake up from. One thing is clear, though; these three dreams have been the most exciting and intense one hour experiences of my life so far."

"This has been the most amazing day of my life, too!" Nan responded. "I've also been searching for you all my life, and never knew if you existed. It seems that I never would have found you either without all of this happening and that SOS signal going forward in time. So I say, let's take this slow from here out and see if it's reality, or just my dream in heaven. I've been touched before Ed, but no one has touched my heart before you."

"Nan, please pull over," Ed asked.

She braked and steered the cab to the side of the road, stopping near one of the streetlights. She put the shifter into neutral and pulled the hand brake back. It went click, click, click and stopped. Ed looked Nan in the eyes and she looked back at him. They embraced and kissed a long time, holding each other as tightly as they could. Afterward, they continued to gaze lovingly at each other. Ed gently stroked her hair.

"You know, I think I'm going to like 1952," he said with a smile and twinkle in his eye.

Chapter 22

Brian Edmond had an inkling that something was not quite right. His three calls to confirm coming over to observe Ed on the futon that evening went unreturned. After getting Ed's voice mail for the third time, Brian left the university at one pm and drove over to Ed's condo in Stapleton. Parking in the driveway, he walked to the door, where he rang the bell and knocked at the same time. He turned the doorknob and the door opened. Walking in, he went to the living room and saw the futon at a funny angle; he noticed the makeshift contraption with the jack taped to the back. He walked around the futon to the coffee table and saw the alarm clock and the manila folder. He picked it up and read the words 'For the Love of Nan' written by Ed on the outside. He set it back down.

Brian looked around the condo. He walked to the garage door and opened it. Ed's Explorer was inside. Brian closed the door and walked into the kitchen, where he saw his suitcase standing next to the kitchen table. He went into Ed's bedroom and found nothing disturbed. Returning to the living room, he looked at the contraption attached to the back of the futon.

"So this is his failsafe device," he said. "It looks like it worked, but where are you, Ed?"

Then it hit him.

"You rascal, you engaged the dream last night didn't you!" he exclaimed.

Ed was totally blown away by what he was thinking. Had something terrible happened?

"Holly molly mother of God, did he do it?" Brian shouted.

He grabbed the thick manila folder off the coffee table and ran out to his car, driving as fast as possible to the downtown Denver public library. After parking out front, he ran to the basement reference area and stopped at the desk, panting and out of breath. The attendant came over and stared at him.

"May I help you?" she asked.

"The microfiche for *The Denver Post* for May 1952," Brian barely got out the words as he tried to catch his breath.

"Those issues are certainly popular. Another gentleman looked at them only days ago," she said, walking away. Returning momentarily, she handed the box to Brian.

"All the issues from May through September 1952 are in here," she said.

He replied, "thank you," and walked over to one of the microfiche readers and sat down. He found the fiche for the week ending May 25, 1952, and loaded it into the machine. In seconds he located the May 24, 1952, issue and looked at the headline page.

13 DEAD IN FATAL STAPLETON

AIRFIELD CRASH – 7 SURVIVE

Brian opened the manila folder and thumbed through the copies Ed made until he found the headline page. He pulled it out and glanced at it.

"Well the headline is the same," he mumbled.

Looking back to the screen, Ed began to read the copy for mention of Nan Orland. He stopped when he spotted her name in the list of survivors.

"This can't be," Brian whispered. "I saw her picture and read her obituary."

He moved the fiche to the obituary pages, but the picture of Nan Orland he had seen in the copy at Casey's was not there. He riffled through the folder and found the obituary page he thought he had looked at before, but it had changed and was now identical to the one on the screen. Replacing Nan Orland's obituary was a new one titled:

Joan Lorry, Wife of KIA Soldier Dies in Plane Crash

"Wow," he said out loud.

Others in the reference room looked at him curiously as he leaned back in his chair to think.

"Now how would Ed send me a message across time?"

Brian moved his hand to the microfiche box and found the fiche for June 23, 1952. He loaded it and began a page-by-page review, freezing when he came to the society pages. There was a picture of a bride and groom; it was Ed and Nan's wedding picture. Both were smiling. Ed was giving a thumbs-up sign.

"He did it, he did it" Brian screamed out.

Standing, he turned excitedly to the many people in the reference room who were intently watching him and gave them all a thumbs-up. Applause broke out.

Fade To Black

CHANGED FATE - Author Lance Stouffer Interview with Orange Splash Magazine

March 2010

LITERARY NEWS

WITH CARMEN ROCHELLE

Splash – *Tell us a little about the story?*

Author – *This is a love story that exemplifies the best in romantic time travel novels and is in the same genre as the book Bid Time Return by science fiction writer Richard Matheson, which was made into the 1980 movie classic Somewhere in Time starring Christopher Reeve and Jane Seymour. My central characters, Nan Orland and Ed Drummond, have been unknowingly searching for each other their whole lives, separated only by time. They are finally brought together by the incredible circumstances of a 1952 airplane crash at Denver's Stapleton Airfield.*

Splash – *How did the subject and location of your story come about?*

Author – *I was traveling on business to Denver for several days in May 2007. At the end of my first day I was invited to dinner at Casey's Irish Pub in the new town of Stapleton which I learned was sitting on the old closed Stapleton Airport. I was intrigued by the area and the next evening I came back alone to explore the entire Stapleton redevelopment. Somehow I wound up in front of the old Stapleton Airport control tower amazed that it was still standing. After retiring to catch a 7 am flight the next day I woke up at 2 am dreaming this fantastic story of a man who moves into a new condo built right on top of where a plane crashed and burned 55 years earlier killing 13 people. Eventually he dreams himself back to that day several times. The epiphany process compelled me to begin writing the story down, which I started and finished by the time I got back to Orlando.*

Splash – Did you have all the details of the story handed to you this way?

Author – Heavens no. I have been researching the subject matter conjured up in this story for over one and a half years. I have even had interviews with people gifted with paranormal abilities. Since I am not a professional writer I have also been learning how to get my story ideas down on paper. It is not an easy process to write a book as you know!

Splash – Who would be your ideal reader?

Author – Anyone who enjoys action adventure novels with a large splash of romance and science fiction or paranormal activity tossed in. I barely scratched the surface of all the concepts involved in writing the story, but focused on bringing my central characters together across time against all odds, with a twist of fate also tossed in. As Americans we always like a winner and the underdog overcoming extreme obstacles. If readers like a positive outcome against impossible odds, then this story will make them smile.

Splash –Your Ed Drummond character is especially interesting. His Big Leg Emma bicycle accident somehow tunes his brain to receive that 55 year old "SOS" signal only on his futon. Why can't he see the crash ghosts in his apartment all the time?

Author – Good question. I don't exactly know. I have never personally seen a ghost day or night. I guess Ed's conscious mind blocks that type of vision. Perhaps it's not as fine tuned or sensitive as his dream state mind. Remember, my story is based in Ed's dream state. It is not a haunting or poltergeist event.

Splash – Okay, what is your stories premise, what are you trying to tell the reader?

Author – My story is about love across time and bringing together two people destined for each other. It focuses on character choices and decisions. I have turned Ed's mental time travel gift into a way to rescue his true love knowing full well, at the beginning of his thinking anyway, the impossibility of their ever being together. The unique premise of my story is that a change of fate is possible across time.

Splash – You present your story first as reality, then repeating in dream segments with Ed Drummond getting smarter and ultimately understanding his strange gift after that thorough explanation given by your psychologist character Brian Edmond. Could you explain why you chose this method to cover such meaty topics?

Author – Time. Reader time. We all seek out professional advice when confronted with things we can't understand. Have you read the US tax code lately? Seriously, the Brian Edmond character gives instant credibility, plausibility and believability to the paranormal concepts discussed. Ed has to get fully knowledgeable about his mental gift in just one evenings discussion. Otherwise Ed would have to research all this for a year to become competent himself. Now in the end, Ed goes against Brian's advice to leave the dream alone and turns his knowledge into the ultimate rescue mission across time. He thinks he has the perfect plan to save Nan, however, we know it's flawed, but still root him on!

Splash – Ed thinks he's in total control of his final rescue dream, but that is far from the truth. Did you give him a false sense of invincibility?

Author – I think we're talking about Ed's selfless decision to try and save his true loves life without messing up the grand time continuum we all exist in. He concludes he can't save everyone, but perhaps he can try and squeeze one more person to the living side in 1952. Its wishful thinking on his part to start with and turns out to be true in the end by his transfer to 1952, but not the way he intended.

Splash – I'll buy the 'love across time' concept, but how does Ed get actually get back to 1952? Will anyone reading your book suspend their reality enough to buy into that one? Will they think this is corny, unbelievable, and not possible?

Author – There you said the word possible. Yes anything is possible. I want you to suspend you belief in the impossibility part of all this for a moment. The story has his connection to the SOS message terminated by the punch inflicted on him by Captain Jamison and by his physically being tossed from the plane. Both events he did not plan. I can only guess the intensity of dream three was equal to any waking reality experience Ed ever had. I mean his mind could not differentiate between wakeful reality and the intense dream which was reality to him, only 55 years earlier. He was convinced he could change the dream and change reality at the same time and change the fate of Nan. Breaking the connection, when his mind was across time has unknown consequences. Now, we can only speculate how he wound up back in 1952 and disappeared from 2007, but that's what makes a great story, and this is a great story. From a technical standpoint, maybe it was a worm hole that pulled him back, or a star trek transporter experience, or a HG Wells time machine experience, but it happened proving that love is stronger than fate, in my opinion anyway.

Splash – Do you think your readers would want to go back to 1952, if placed in the same circumstances and they could make it happen?

Author – Now you're getting at the heart of the larger subject and that's escape from our current reality. Well, I know many folks who are not happy with their present circumstances and can't seem to break-out from where they are to where they want to be. Perhaps life has taken them in a direction they regret or wish they could change, but know they can't. So you ask me if there is someone on this planet who would gladly give up everything for a one way trip to the past and I would have to say, yes, those persons exist. I suggest you pole your readers to see who would like a one-way ticket to 1952 or 1957 or 1965. You may be amazed!

Splash – Interesting analysis of the possibilities of going back in time. You mention many things in the book, but your title, I guess says it all. Can you elaborate on changing fate?

Author – Sure, I have an opinion on just about everything, including fate. I have been trying to determine if fate is male, female or God. Is it good or evil? Do you know for sure what it is? One thing I have concluded in my research of the subject is that fate is pretty much the status quo. Meaning, when fate is known, fate, whoever, or whatever it is, does not like being changed. Especially meddling with the past, which my interloper character Ed Drummond does. One thing is clear you can't cheat fate. No way can that happen. Again I accept fate, but think it can possibly be bent, which this story certainly does.

Splash – Tell us a little about yourself.

Author – Okay, my day job is as a CPA and financial consultant to the construction equipment industry, which I have been in for almost thirty years. My night pastime and joy is writer, author and publisher. This is my second book, the first was a children's book Ode to Miss Jasmine Cat which was featured in CAT FANCY MAGAZINE. As you see I do not have the typical writer's profile.

Splash – Anything you wish to add to our conversation today?

Author – Rescue missions are heroic. Answering a SOS call across time and attempting a rescue mission takes kahunas. Can I say that? I wrote this book for all you lovers and dreamers that can see all the possibilities out there with a smile! You will thoroughly enjoy Changed Fate.

*SINGAPORE GOLD is the first novel in the '**TOSA** files' series featuring mastermind Australian Soldier of Fortune Dickey Kincaid, British flying bombshell Trish Matthews, American World War II pilot extraordinaire Cat McCoy, the sultry and mysterious Jasmine Chen, joker Capitaine Jadot of the French Foreign Legion and war hero Colonel Dusant of the French Army.*

FORMATS - Paperback, Kindle, Nook
Visit www.heathrowpublishing.com for more information

RETURNING IN 2013

Stay tuned for the next action packed adventure of the ***TOSA*** files series featuring mastermind Australian Soldier of Fortune Dickey Kincaid, British flying bombshell Trish Matthews, American World War II pilot extraordinaire Cat McCoy, the sultry and mysterious Jasmine Chen, joker Capitaine Jadot of the French Foreign Legion and war hero Colonel Dusant of the French Army who will all return in;

INDO CHINA 53

A *TOSA* FILES NOVEL

"Heads up….If we don't act fast…..everybody dies."

www.heathrowpublishing.com

12547710R00082

Made in the USA
Charleston, SC
12 May 2012